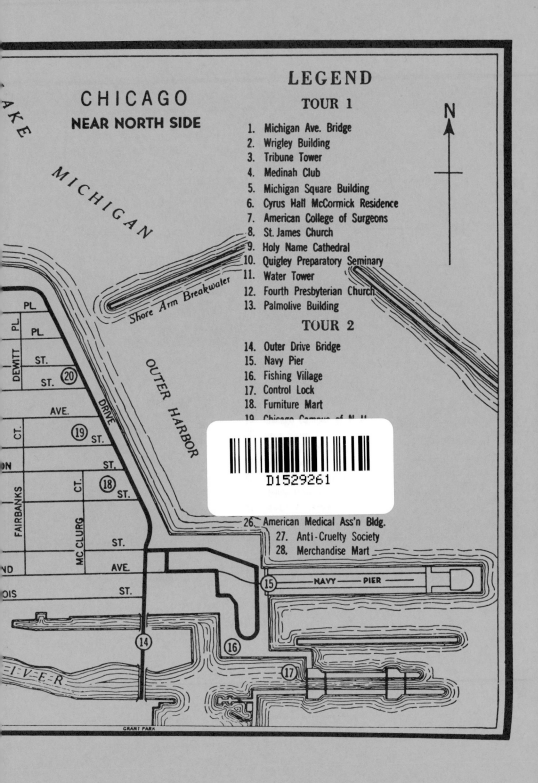

CHICAGO
NEAR NORTH SIDE

LEGEND

TOUR 1

1. Michigan Ave. Bridge
2. Wrigley Building
3. Tribune Tower
4. Medinah Club
5. Michigan Square Building
6. Cyrus Hall McCormick Residence
7. American College of Surgeons
8. St. James Church
9. Holy Name Cathedral
10. Quigley Preparatory Seminary
11. Water Tower
12. Fourth Presbyterian Church
13. Palmolive Building

TOUR 2

14. Outer Drive Bridge
15. Navy Pier
16. Fishing Village
17. Control Lock
18. Furniture Mart
19. Chicago Campus of N. U.

26. American Medical Ass'n Bldg.
27. Anti-Cruelty Society
28. Merchandise Mart

N

LAKE

MICHIGAN

Shore Arm Breakwater

OUTER HARBOR

OUTER DRIVE

NAVY — PIER

GRANT PARK

A GOOD MAN
TO KNOW

A GOOD
MAN TO KNOW

A Semi-Documentary
Fictional Memoir

BARRY GIFFORD

CLARK CITY PRESS
LIVINGSTON · MONTANA

LIBRARY OF CONGRESS CATALOGING-IN-PUBLICATION DATA

GIFFORD, BARRY, 1946–
   A GOOD MAN TO KNOW: A SEMI-DOCUMENTARY FICTIONAL MEMOIR /
BARRY GIFFORD.
   P. CM.
ISBN 0-944439-36-5
   I. FICTION   I. TITLE.
PS3557.1283G6 1992   813.54   QBI92-126   91-58688

FIRST EDITION

Parts of this book, mostly in different form, have appeared in the *Arizona Republic*, *Cassette Gazette*, *Creative States*, *Chicago Tribune*, *Western American Literature*, *The National Pastime*, *The Minneapolis Review of Baseball*, *The Temple of Baseball*, *The Berkeley Monthly*, *Mystery Scene*, *Response*, *San Francisco Chronicle*, *Smoke Signals*, *The Emil Verban Memorial Society Newsletter*, *California Living (San Francisco Examiner)*, *Image (San Francisco Examiner)*, *Rolling Stock*, *Periodics*, *The Second Black Lizard Anthology of Crime Fiction*, *El País* (Madrid), *The San Francisco Review of Books* and *The Fireside Book of Baseball*. The title chapter, "A Good Man to Know," received a PEN Syndicated Fiction Award and was included in *The Available Press/PEN Short Story Collection* (New York: Ballantine Books, 1985).

The author is grateful to the PEN American Center and the National Endowment for the Arts Literature Program for their support extended through the PEN Syndicated Fiction Project.

The author wishes also to acknowledge the cooperation and assistance of James K. Hall, Chief, Freedom of Information–Privacy Acts Section, Records Management Division, United States Department of Justice, Federal Bureau of Investigation, Washington, D.C.; and Detective Elliot Mathews and Gladys Lindsay, Director of News Affairs, Chicago Police Headquarters, Chicago, Illinois. Their diligence in helping to provide documents relevant to the subject of this book is greatly appreciated. Thanks also to Michael M. Conway, Paul Ostrof and Edith Biller.

FOR MARK

AND IN HOMAGE TO NELSON ALGREN, WHO
WROTE, "THE CHICAGO OF THE NINETEEN-FORTIES
IS UNRECORDED AND THAT OF THE FIFTIES IS SUNK
FOR KEEPS."

BOOKS BY BARRY GIFFORD

FICTION

The Sailor & Lula Novels:
  Wild at Heart
  59° and Raining
  Sailor's Holiday
  Sultans of Africa
  Consuelo's Kiss
  Bad Day for the Leopard Man
A Good Man to Know
New Mysteries of Paris
Port Tropique
An Unfortunate Woman
Landscape with Traveler
A Boy's Novel

NONFICTION

A Day at the Races
The Devil Thumbs a Ride
The Neighborhood of Baseball
Saroyan: A Biography (with Lawrence Lee)
Jack's Book: An Oral Biography of Jack Kerouac (with Lawrence Lee)

POETRY

Ghosts No Horses Can Carry
Giotto's Circle
Beautiful Phantoms
Persimmons: Poems for Paintings
The Boy You Have Always Loved
Poems from Snail Hut
Horse Hauling Timber from Hokkaido Forest
Coyote Tantras
The Blood of the Parade

TRANSLATIONS

Selected Poems of Francis Jammes (with Bettina Dickie)

The father, dead very early . . . merely touched the surface of childhood with an almost silent bounty.
—ROLAND BARTHES

When I met [Meyer Lansky and Doc Stracher] by chance in the lobby of the Tel Aviv Sheraton . . . I was caused to blurt: 'Gentlemen, it's like meeting Ruth and Gehrig.'
—SIDNEY ZION

AUTHOR'S NOTE

The Japanese form shōsetsu *is defined by the eminent translator* (The Tale of Genji, The Makioka Sisters, *etc.) Edward Seidensticker as "a piece of autobiography or a set of memoirs, somewhat embroidered and colored but essentially nonfiction." Yasunari Kawabata considered his "faithful chronicle-novel"* The Master of Go *to be in the realm of* shōsetsu. *As Mr. Seidensticker has noted, while* shōsetsu *contains elements of fiction, it is "a rather more flexible and generous and catholic term than 'novel.' "* A Good Man to Know *belongs to the genre of* shōsetsu *and should be approached as such by the reader.*

—B. G.

CONTENTS

A GOOD MAN
TO KNOW

A Good Man to Know

I was seven years old in June of 1954 when my dad and I drove from Miami to New Orleans to visit his friend Albert Thibodeaux. It was a cloudy, humid morning when we rolled into town in my dad's powder blue Cadillac. The river smell mixed with malt from the Jax brewery and the smoke from my dad's chain of Lucky Strikes to give the air an odor of toasted heat. We parked the car by Jackson Square and walked over a block to Tujague's bar to meet Albert. "It feels like it's going to rain," I said to Dad. "It always feels like this in New Orleans," he said.

Albert Thibodeaux was a gambler. In the evenings he presided over cockfights and pit-bull matches across the river in Gretna or Algiers but during the day he hung out at Tujague's on Decatur Street with the railroad men and phony artists from the Quarter. He and my dad knew each other from the old days in Cuba, which I knew nothing about except that they'd both lived at the Nacional in Havana.

According to Nanny, my mother's mother, my dad didn't even speak to me until I was five years old. He apparently didn't consider a child capable of understanding him or a friendship worth cultivating until that age and he may have been correct in his judgment. I certainly never felt deprived as a result of this policy. If my grandmother hadn't told me about it I would have never known the difference.

My dad never really told me about what he did or had done before I was old enough to go around with him. I picked up information as I went, listening to guys like Albert and some of my dad's other friends like Willie Nero in Chicago and Dummy Fish in New York. We supposedly lived in Chicago but my dad had places in Miami, New York and Acapulco. We traveled, mostly without my mother who stayed at the house in Chicago and went to church a lot. Once I asked my dad if we were any particular religion and he said, "Your mother's a Catholic."

Albert was a short, fat man with a handlebar mustache. He looked like a Maxwell Street organ grinder without the organ or the monkey. He and my dad drank Irish whisky from ten in the morning until lunchtime, which was around one-thirty, when they sent me down to the Central Grocery on Decatur or to Johnny's on St. Louis Street for muffaletas. I brought back three of them but Albert and Dad didn't eat theirs. They just talked and once in a while Albert went into the back to make a phone call. They got along just fine and about once an hour Albert would ask if I wanted something, like a Barq's or a Delaware Punch, and Dad would rub my shoulder and say to Albert, "He's a real piece of meat, this boy." Then Albert would grin so that his mustache covered the front of his nose and say, "He is, Rudy. You won't want to worry about him."

When Dad and I were in New York one night I heard him talking in a loud voice to Dummy Fish in the lobby of the Waldorf. I was sitting in a big leather chair between a sand-filled ashtray and a potted palm and Dad came over and told me that Dummy would take me upstairs to our room. I should go to sleep, he said, he'd be back late. In the elevator I looked at Dummy and saw that he was sweating. It was December but water ran down from his temples to his chin. "Does my dad have a job?" I asked Dummy. "Sure he does," he said. "Of course. Your dad has to work, just like everybody else." "What is it?" I asked. Dummy wiped the sweat from his face with a white and blue checkered handkerchief. "He talks to people," Dummy told me. "Your dad is a great talker."

Dad and Albert talked right past lunchtime and I must have fallen asleep on the bar because when I woke up it was dark out and I was in the back seat of the car. We were driving across the Huey P. Long Bridge and a freight train was running along the tracks over our heads. "How about some Italian oysters, son?" my dad asked. "We'll stop up here in Houma and get some cold beer and dinner." We were cruising in the passing lane in the powder blue Caddy over the big brown river. Through the bridge railings I watched the barge lights twinkle as they inched ahead through the water.

"Albert's a businessman, the best kind." Dad lit a fresh Lucky from an old one and threw the butt out the window. "He's a good man to know, remember that."

The Old Country

My grandfather never wore an overcoat. That was Ezra, my father's father, who had a candy stand under the Addison Street elevated tracks near Wrigley Field. Even in winter, when it was ten below and the wind cut through the station, Ezra never wore more than a heavy sport coat, and sometimes, when Aunt Belle, his second wife, insisted, a woolen scarf wrapped up around his chin. He was six-foot-two and two hundred pounds, had his upper lip covered by a bushy mustache, and a full head of dark hair until he died at ninety, not missing a day at his stand till six months before.

He never told anyone his business. He ran numbers from the stand and owned an apartment building on the South Side. He outlived three wives and one of his sons, my father. His older son, my Uncle Bruno, looked just like him, but Bruno was mean and defensive whereas Ezra was brusque but kind. He always gave me and my friends gum or candy on our way to and from the ballpark, and he liked me to hang around there or at another stand he had for a while at Belmont Avenue, especially on Saturdays so he could show me off to his regular cronies. He'd put me on a box behind the stand and keep one big hand on my shoulder. "This is my *grandson*," he'd say, and wait until he was sure they had looked at me. I was the first and then his only grandson; Uncle Bruno had two girls. "Good *boy*!"

He left it to his sons to make the big money, and they did all right, my dad with the rackets and the liquor store, Uncle Bruno as an auctioneer, but they never had to take care of the old man, he took care of himself.

Ezra spoke broken English; he came to America with his sons (my dad was seven, Bruno fourteen) and a daughter from Vienna in 1918. I always remember him standing under the tracks outside the station in February, cigar stub poked out between mustache and muffler, waiting for me and my dad to pick him up. When we'd pull up along the curb my dad would honk but the old man wouldn't notice. I would always have to run out and get him. I figured Ezra always saw us but waited for me to come for him. It made him feel better if I got out and grabbed his hand and led him to the car.

"Pa, for Chrissakes, why don't you wear an overcoat?" my dad would ask. "It's cold."

The old man wouldn't look over or answer right away. He'd sit with me on his lap as my father pointed the car into the dark.

"What cold?" he'd say after we'd gone a block or two. "In the *old* country was cold."

Mrs. Kashfi

My mother has always been a great believer in fortune-tellers, a predilection my dad considered as bizarre as her devotion to the Catholic church. He refused even to discuss anything having to do with either entity, a policy that seemed only to reinforce my mother's arcane quest. Even now she informs me whenever she's stumbled upon a seer whose prognostications strike her as being particularly apt. I once heard my dad describe her as belonging to "the sisterhood of the Perpetual Pursuit of the Good Word."

My own experience with fortune-tellers is limited to what I observed as a small boy, when I had no choice but to accompany my mother on her frequent pilgrimages to Mrs. Kashfi. Mrs. Kashfi was a tea-leaf reader who lived with her bird in a two-room apartment in a large gray brick building on Hollywood Avenue in Chicago. As soon as we entered the downstairs lobby the stuffiness of the place began to overwhelm me. It was as if Mrs. Kashfi lived in a vault to which no fresh air was admitted. The lobby, elevator and hallways were suffocating, too hot both in summer, when there was too little ventilation, and in winter, when the building was unbearably overheated. And the whole place stank terribly, as if no food other than boiled cabbage were allowed to be prepared. My mother, who was usually all too aware of these sorts of unappealing aspects, seemed blissfully unaware of them at Mrs.

Kashfi's. The oracle was in residence, and that was all that mattered.

The worst olfactory assault, however, came from Mrs. Kashfi's apartment, in the front room where her bird, a blind, practically featherless dinge-yellow parakeet, was kept and whose cage Mrs. Kashfi failed to clean with any regularity. It was in that room, on a lumpy couch with dirt-gray lace doily arm covers, that I was made to wait for my mother while she and Mrs. Kashfi, locked in the inner sanctum of the bedroom, voyaged into the sea of clairvoyance.

The apartment was filled with overstuffed chairs and couches, dressers crowded with bric-a-brac and framed photographs of strangely dressed, stiff and staring figures, relics of the old country which to me appeared as evidence of extraterrestrial existence. Nothing seemed quite real, as if with a snap of Mrs. Kashfi's sorceress's fingers the entire scene would disappear. Mrs. Kashfi herself was a small, very old woman who was permanently bent slightly forwards so that she appeared about to topple over, causing me to avoid allowing her to hover over me for longer than a moment. She had a large nose and she wore glasses, as well as two or more dark green or brown sweaters at all times, despite the already hellish climate.

I dutifully sat on the couch, listening to the murmurings from beyond the bedroom door, and to the blind bird drop pelletlike feces onto the stained newspaper in its filthy cage. No sound issued from the parakeet's enclosure other than the constant "tup, tup" of its evacuation. Behind the bird cage was a weather-smeared window, covered with eyelet curtains, that looked out on the brick wall of another building.

I stayed put on the couch and waited for my mother's session to end. Each visit lasted about a half hour, at the finish of which

Mrs. Kashfi would walk my mother to the doorway, where they'd stand and talk for another ten minutes while I fidgeted in the smelly hall trying to see how long I could hold my breath.

Only once did I have a glimpse of the mundane evidence from which Mrs. Kashfi made her miraculous analysis. At the conclusion of a session my mother came out of the bedroom carrying a teacup, which she told me to look into.

"What does it mean?" I asked.

"Your grandmother is safe and happy," my mother said.

My grandmother, my mother's mother, had recently died, so this news puzzled me. I looked again at the brown bits in the bottom of the china cup. Mrs. Kashfi came over and leaned above me, nodding her big nose with long hairs in the nostrils. I moved away and waited by the door, wondering what my dad would have thought of all this, while my mother stood smiling, staring into the cup.

The Piano Lesson

I bounced the ball against the yellow wall in the front of my house, waiting for the piano teacher. I'd been taking lessons for six weeks and I liked the piano, my mother played well, standards and show tunes, and sang. Often I sang along with her or by myself as she played. "Young at Heart" and "Bewitched, Bothered and Bewildered" were two of my favorites. I loved the dark blue cover of the sheet music of "Bewitched," with the drawing of the woman in a flowing white gown in the lower left-hand corner. It made me think of New York, though I'd never been there. White on midnight dark.

I liked to stand next to the piano bench while my mother played and listen to "Satan Takes a Holiday," a fox-trot it said on the sheet music. I was eight years old and could easily imagine foxes trotting in evening gowns.

I was up to "The Scissors-Grinder" and "Swan on the Lake" in the second red Thompson book. That was pretty good for six weeks, but I had begun to stutter. I knew I had begun to stutter because I'd heard my mother say it to my father on the phone. They ought just to ignore it, she'd said, and it would stop.

"Ready for your lesson today?" asked the teacher as she came up the walk.

"I'll be in in a minute," I said, continuing to bounce the ball off the yellow bricks. The teacher smiled and went into the building.

I kept hitting the ball against the wall. I knew she would be talking to my mother, then arranging the lesson books on the rack above the piano. I hit the ball once high above the first-floor windows, caught it and ran.

A Rainy Day at the Nortown Theater

When I was about nine or ten years old my dad picked me up from school one day and took me to the movies. I didn't see him very often since my parents were divorced and I lived with my mother. This day my dad asked me what I wanted to do and since it was raining hard we decided to go see *Dragnet* starring Jack Webb and an Alan Ladd picture, *Shane*.

During the show my dad bought me a Holloway Slo-Poke caramel sucker and buttered popcorn. I had already seen *Dragnet* twice and since it wasn't such a great movie I was really interested in seeing *Shane*, which I'd already seen as well, but only once, and had liked it, especially the end where the kid, Brandon DeWilde, goes running through the bullrushes calling for Shane to come back, "Come back, Shane! Shane, come back!" I had really remembered that scene and was anxious to see it again, so all during *Dragnet* I kept still because I thought my dad wanted to see it, not having already seen it, and when *Shane* came on I was happy.

But it was Wednesday and my dad had promised my mother he'd have me home for dinner at six, so at about a quarter to, like I had dreaded in the back of my head, my dad said we had to go.

"But Dad," I said, "*Shane*'s not over till six-thirty and I want to see the end where the kid goes running after him yelling, 'Come back, Shane!' That's the best part!"

But my dad said no, we had to go, so I got up and went with

him but walked slowly backwards up the aisle to see as much of the picture as I could even though I knew now I wasn't going to get to see the end, and we were in the lobby which was dark and red with gold curtains and saw it was still pouring outside. My dad made me put on my coat and duck my head down into it when we made a run for the car which was parked not very far away.

My dad drove me home and talked to me but I didn't hear what he said. I was thinking about the kid who would be running after Shane in about ten more minutes. I kissed my dad good-bye and went in to eat dinner but I stood in the hall and watched him drive off before I did.

The Mason-Dixon Line

One Sunday I accompanied my dad on an automobile trip up from Chicago to Dixon, Illinois. It was a sunny January morning, and it must have been when I was ten years old because I remember that I wore the black leather motorcycle jacket I'd received that Christmas. I was very fond of that jacket with its multitude of bright silver zippers and two silver stars on each epaulet. I also wore a blue cashmere scarf of my dad's and an old pair of brown leather gloves he'd given me after my mother gave him a new pair of calfskins for Christmas.

I liked watching the snowy fields as we sped past them on the narrow, two-lane northern Illinois roads. We passed through a number of little towns, each of them with seemingly identical centers: a Rexall, hardware store, First State Bank of Illinois, Presbyterian, Methodist and Catholic churches with snow-capped steeples, and a statue of Black Hawk, the heroic Sac and Fox chief.

When my dad had asked me if I wanted to take a ride with him that morning I'd said sure, without asking where to or why. My dad never asked twice and he never made any promises about when we'd be back. I liked the uncertainty of those situations, the open-endedness about them. Anything could happen, I figured; it was more fun not knowing what to expect.

"We're going to Dixon," Dad said after we'd been driving for about forty-five minutes. "To see a man named Mason." I'd recently read a Young Readers biography of Robert E. Lee, so I knew all about the Civil War. "We're on the Mason-Dixon Line," I said, and laughed, pleased with my little kid's idea of a joke. "That's it, boy," said my dad. "We're going to get a line on Mason in Dixon."

The town of Dixon appeared to be one street long, like in a western movie: the hardware store, bank, church and drugstore. I didn't see a statue. We went into a tiny cafe next to the bank that was empty except for a counterman. Dad told me to sit in one of the booths and told the counterman to give me a hot chocolate and whatever else I wanted.

"I'll be back in an hour, son," said Dad. He gave the counterman a twenty-dollar bill and walked out. When the counterman brought over the hot chocolate he asked if there was anything else he could get for me. "A hamburger," I said, "and an order of fries." "You got it," he said.

I sipped slowly at the hot chocolate until he brought me the hamburger and fries. The counterman sat on a stool near the booth and looked at me. "That your old man?" he asked. "He's my dad," I said, between bites of the hamburger. "Any special reason he's here?" he asked. I didn't say anything and the counterman said, "You are from Chi, aren't ya?" I nodded yes and kept chewing. "You must be here for a reason," he said. "My dad needs to see someone," I said. "Thought so," said the counterman. "Know his name?" I took a big bite of the hamburger before I answered. "No," I said. The counterman looked at me, then out the window again. After a minute he walked over behind the counter. "Let me know if ya need anything else," he said.

While my dad was gone I tried to imagine who this fellow Mason was. I figured he must be some guy hiding out from the Chicago cops, and that his real name probably wasn't Mason. My dad came back in less than an hour, picked up his change from the counterman, tipped him and said to me, "Had enough to eat?" I said yes and followed him out to the car.

"This is an awfully small town," I said to my dad as we drove away. "Does Mason live here?" "Who?" he asked. Then he said, "Oh yeah, Mason." Dad didn't say anything else for a while. He took a cigar out of his overcoat pocket, bit off the tip, rolled down his window and spit it out before saying, "No, he doesn't live here. Just visiting."

We drove along for a few miles before Dad lit his cigar, leaving the window open. I put the scarf up around my face to keep warm and settled back in the seat. My dad drove and didn't talk for about a half hour. Around Marengo he said, "Did that counterman back there ask you any questions?" "He asked me if you were my dad and if we were from Chicago," I said. "What did you tell him?" "I said yes." "Anything else?" "He asked if you were there for any special reason and I said you were there to see someone." "Did you tell him who?" Dad asked. "I said I didn't know his name."

Dad nodded and threw his dead cigar out the window, then rolled it up. "You tired?" he asked. "No," I said. "What do you think," he said, "would you rather live out here or in the city?" "The city," I said. "I think it's more interesting there." "So do I," said Dad. "Relax, son, and we'll be home before you know it."

An Eye on the Alligators

I knew as the boat pulled in to the dock there were no alligators out there. I got up and stuck my foot against the piling so that it wouldn't scrape the boat, then got out and secured the bow line to the nearest cleat. Mr. Reed was standing on the dock now, helping my mother up out of the boat. Her brown legs came up off the edge weakly, so that Mr. Reed had to lift her to keep her from falling back. The water by the pier was blue-black and stank of oil and gas, not like out on the ocean, or in the channel, where we had been that day.

Mr. Reed had told me to watch for the alligators. The best spot to do it from, he said, was up on the bow. So I crawled up through the trap door on the bow and watched for the alligators. The river water was clear and green.

"Look around the rocks," Mr. Reed shouted over the engine noise, "the gators like the rocks." So I kept my eye on the rocks, but there were no alligators.

"I don't see any," I shouted. "Maybe we're going too fast and the noise scares them away."

After that Mr. Reed went slower but still there were no alligators. We were out for nearly three hours and I didn't see one.

"It was just a bad day for seeing alligators, son," said Mr. Reed. "Probably because of the rain. They don't like to come up when it's raining."

For some reason I didn't like it when Mr. Reed called me "son." I wasn't his son. Mr. Reed, my mother told me, was a friend of my father's. My dad was not in Florida with us, he was in Chicago doing business while my mother and I rode around in boats and visited alligator farms.

Mr. Reed had one arm around me and one arm around my mother.

"Can we go back out tomorrow?" I asked.

My mother laughed. "That's up to Mr. Reed," she said. "We don't want to impose on him too much."

"Sure, kid," said Mr. Reed. Then he laughed, too.

I looked up at Mr. Reed, then out at the water. I could see the drops disappearing into their holes on the surface.

Letter from Larry

Hello Boy—

Thank you for your nice letter. Youse guys must have been eating too much candy! Huh? That's the reason the candy was taken away. Yes? No? I'll betcha!!

Also—it's good to hear that you have rid yourself of that cold, and you now feel "very good."

We, here at home, miss you. But, we hope you are at least having some fun. Otherwise, the whole deal is "No Good." How about it?

Mother tells me that she wrote a note to you today, and in it she told you about our sailing trip with your Uncle Buck. But—I don't think your mother gave you all the "horrible" details. So—I shall do so!—Are you listening, Boy?

First, let me tell you that Uncle Buck has a beaut of a sailboat. It's really keen! It's 27 feet long, has a real high mast, which carries a big spread of mainsail—and also a high jib sail. This boat was made in Sweden—and it can really travel fast.

Well, 2 Sundays ago—Mother, Pops and I went sailing on the "Friendship" (that's the name of the boat) with Uncle Buck. It was too calm (no breeze) for fast sailing, so we just "horsed around" the lake for the afternoon without any danger or excitement.

But—yesterday (Sunday) we went sailing again! There was your cousin Darlene and her boyfriend, Chris and Uncle Buck and Mother and I.

It looked sort of rough on the lake. The waves were high, and there was a strong Northeast wind.—But—in spite of all that we went out—and man—it was rough!

We had full sails on. I was up forward hanging on a mast stay for dear life, and the waves kept coming over the deck, soaking me from head to feet. Of course, all I wore was bathing shorts.

The wind kept us keeled over, so that one side of the boat was high up and the other side was under the water. It sorta scared Mother, a bit—And I'll tell you a secret, it scared me too, tho I'll never admit it!

It kept getting rougher and rougher. We saw another sailboat ram into a cabin cruiser, snapping the mast—and they had to be rescued.

Anyway boy, there were a few times I thought I'd fall in the water. But—I hung on with a leg wrapped around a stay.

Finally, one of the mast stays broke—and we were lucky to have the wind on our side, because we had to take down all the sails, and the wind blew us towards the harbor, where we got a tow to our anchorage. It was a rough trip—But all's well that ends well.

Mom has a cold from the windy trip—But, we will see that she shakes it off.

The McLaughlin kids say "Hello." They want to know when you are getting back here.

All's well, son. Take care of yourself.

> *Our Love To You*
> *Your*
> *Larr*

I read the letter over and over. It was written to me when I was about eight or nine while I was up in Wisconsin at summer camp by my mother's second husband, Larry. It's a horrible story. They were married six months; he was tall and handsome, an Irishman, Lucius Larry Cohan, George M. Cohan's nephew, he said.

I really loved him. Not the same as the way I loved my dad, but he and I played together all the time; he never had to discipline me, I always did what Larry wanted because he was such a great guy, and I knew my mother loved him because he was so handsome and smart. A great athlete, trim and hard, Larry was nearly fifty, maybe more, but looked ten or more years younger. We were really happy, my mother and Larry and I, during this six months.

Then one day Larry refused to get out of bed. Like Bartleby, he just preferred not to get up. My mother went running out to our cousins' house semi-hysterical, absolutely at a loss as to what to do. I was home sick from school that day. I sat in the room and watched him. Larry just lay there. When people came to talk to him he would nod, or just whisper a wistful "No."

He stared, not vacantly, but mournfully, an eerie but not frightening—to me, anyway—saddened stare, like *he knew*. Not in any hierarchical sense, but as if he felt there was nothing to do but lie there, looking up at the ceiling. Finally my mother took me away and told me to stay in another room.

I didn't know what was happening. Eventually my mother made Larry leave, forced him to slowly put on socks and pants and shirt and shoes and walk out. He did it as if he were in a dream, in dream-motion, not really there at all. He was vapor; standing, walking, even lying there was some irreality, not conscious action. He was looking around for the angels.

My mother later found out from Larry's sister in Charleston, West Virginia, that he had been wounded and shell-shocked in the war. He had married my mother after being released from the VA hospital, never told her, and had a metal plate in his head. He wasn't allowed to drive because of it.

He went to stay in The Cass, a run-down fleabag hotel on the Near North Side of Chicago. My mother and I picked him up there one day and we went to the park. Larry begged my mother to take him back, that he'd be all right; and she was tempted because he was so handsome and all, but now weak and vague and unshaven, obviously struggling terribly. Even I, at eight years old, could see this.

I was half-frightened of him then because of his strange, bedraggled appearance and lost-soul incoherence. We were going to lunch, walking to the restaurant, and Larry said, "Where are we going now?" My mother said, "We're going to the restaurant to eat lunch, like you suggested." "That's a good idea," Larry said, "let's go eat lunch."

Naturally this scared my mother, who was still young, only twenty-nine, and under the thumb of relatives in those days who were warning her, telling her not to take him back. (Many were just jealous because, when sane, Larry was so sharp, too fast for them and made them uncomfortable. Also, his handsomeness disturbed my mother's ugly women relatives, who were envious.) So, my mother divorced him, and I never saw him again.

The Aerodynamics of an Irishman

There was a man who lived on my block when I was a kid whose name was Rooney Sullavan. He would often come walking down the street while the kids were playing ball in front of my house or Johnny McLaughlin's house. Rooney would always stop and ask if he'd ever shown us how he used to throw the knuckleball back when he pitched for Kankakee in 1930.

"Plenty of times, Rooney," Billy Cunningham would say. "No knuckles about it, right?" Tommy Ryan would say. "No knuckles about it, right!" Rooney Sullavan would say. "Give it here and I'll show you." One of us would reluctantly toss Rooney the ball and we'd step up so he could demonstrate for the fortieth time how he held the ball by his fingertips only, no knuckles about it.

"Don't know how it ever got the name knuckler," Rooney'd say. "I call mine the Rooneyball." Then he'd tell one of us, usually Billy because he had the catcher's glove—the old fat-heeled kind that didn't bend unless somebody stepped on it, a big black mitt that Billy's dad had handed down to him from *his* days at Kankakee or Rock Island or someplace—to get sixty feet away so Rooney could see if he could still "make it wrinkle."

Billy would pace off twelve squares of sidewalk, each square being approximately five feet long, the length of one nine-year-old boy's body stretched head to toe lying flat, squat down and stick his big black glove out in front of his face. With his right hand he'd cover his crotch in case the pitch got away and short-hopped off the cement where he couldn't block it with the mitt. The knuckleball was unpredictable, not even Rooney could tell what would happen once he let it go.

"It's the air makes it hop," Rooney claimed. His leather jacket creaked as he bent, wound up, rotated his right arm like nobody'd done since Chief Bender, crossed his runny grey eyes and released the ball from the tips of his fingers. We watched as it sailed straight up at first then sort of floated on an invisible wave before plunging the last ten feet like a balloon that had been pierced by a dart.

Billy always went down on his knees, the back of his right hand stiffened over his crotch, and stuck out his gloved hand at the slowly whirling Rooneyball. Just before it got to Billy's mitt the ball would give out entirely and sink rapidly, inducing Billy to lean forward in order to catch it, only he couldn't because at the last instant it would take a final, sneaky hop before bouncing surprisingly hard off of Billy's unprotected chest.

"*Just* like I told you," Rooney Sullavan would exclaim. "All it takes is plain old air."

Billy would come up with the ball in his upturned glove, his right hand rubbing the place on his chest where the pitch had hit. "You all right, son?" Rooney would ask, and Billy would nod. "Tough kid," Rooney'd say. "I'd like to stay out with you fellas all day, but I got responsibilities." Rooney would muss up Billy's hair with the hand that held the secret to the Rooneyball and walk away whistling "When Irish Eyes Are Smiling" or "My Wild Irish Rose." Rooney was about forty-five or fifty years old and lived with his mother in a bungalow at the corner. He worked nights for Wanzer Dairy, washing out returned milk bottles.

Tommy Ryan would grab the ball out of Billy's mitt and hold it by the tips of his fingers like Rooney Sullavan did, and Billy would go sit on the stoop in front of the closest house and rub his chest. "No way," Tommy would say, considering the prospect of his ever duplicating Rooney's feat. "There must be something he's not telling us."

The Back to School Blacks and Blues

My dad never knew what I went through in school while he was alive and I'm glad he didn't. I never talked about it, he never asked, and it was just as well. I don't know what he would have done. The worst day of school was always the first. In Chicago we usually went back to school the first day after Labor Day. The weather was still good and it was something of a shock to the system—both physiologically and psychologically—to all of a sudden be cooped up in a stuffy classroom after two and a half months of virtually unmitigated freedom. Even if a kid worked a summer job it wasn't the same as being confined in a tomblike enclosure along with thirty or forty other suffering, sweating, restless prisoners of the Board of Education while a teacher barked away, oblivious to your discomfort.

I have three distinct memories of the occasion, that excruciatingly difficult reentry to pedagogic reality. On the first day of fifth grade, in the middle of the afternoon, Mr. Mooth, the head maintenance man and janitor of DeWitt Clinton Grammar School, a San Quentinlike institution built a few minutes after the Fall of Rome, came into our room and without saying a word to the teacher told all of the boys to stand up next to their seat. Herman Mooth was a large man in his fifties who'd been the janitor and boiler-room mechanic at Clinton School for thirty years. He always wore the same clothes: a woolen checked shirt, baggy brown bum pants held up by suspenders, and steel-toed park ranger shoes. In one back pocket he had a crumpled, filthy grey handkerchief half sticking out and in the other he carried a dark brown half-pint bottle of rye whisky. He had a grizzled grey mustache with hair to match—always worn a little bit too long, which in those days, the mid-fifties, was considered eccentric—and a perpetual scowl. All of the kids were afraid of him—the teachers probably were, too—and we stayed out of his way when he walked across the school yard from the maintenance shack to the main building. Rumor had it that Mooth had once caught a little kid who'd thrown a snowball at his head and held him upside down in front of the open school coal-furnace door for an hour before letting him go. Mr. Mooth never wore a coat, not even when it was ten or twenty degrees below zero in the middle of February; and in the hot months he always wore the same long-sleeved woolen shirt with the cuffs unbuttoned. So when Mooth came into our room that hot, sticky September day in 1957 everyone, even Miss Lawson, our classic old maid-type teacher, was taken aback.

"You, you and you!" Mooth shouted at three of us boys, including me. "You stand! The others sit!" he commanded. Pointing a stubby, swollen index finger at us he said, "I saw you three punks smoking in the school yard at eight o' clock last night. This is private property. If I catch you little jerks here again I'll get you sent to Bridewell"—the juvenile prison—"You got me?" The room was silent, nobody moved. Mooth stood there, pointing that grease-stained digit at us, his little red eyes boiling in the sunny classroom. I could see the dust motes floating past them. Then I spoke, "That wasn't me, Mr. Mooth," I said. "I wasn't in the school yard last night. And I don't smoke."

Mooth moved with the speed of a panther. He was at my desk before I knew what was happening and he slapped me hard across the face. "Don't!" he bellowed at me, sticking his flat fingertip into my chest. "Don't lie to me! I saw you! I can't prove it but you and your punk pals were smoking. I got all the butts as evidence!" Every eye in the classroom was on me. I didn't move one hair on my not yet eleven-year-old head. Mooth stood in front of me for a full minute or more, breathing heavily, his whisky breath blasting its way up my nostrils. I stopped breathing. Suddenly Mooth turned and walked out, slamming the door behind him. Old Miss Lawson, who was tall and skinny and wore a black dress every day, stared hard at me through her thick spectacles. I was branded in her eyes as a Bad Kid. Nothing I could say or do would dig me out of the hole Mr. Mooth had shoved me into. I knew that year would be a long haul, and it was. I never had a chance.

My second and third most vivid memories of back to school adventures both occurred on the same day, my first day of high school. I was sitting in the first row, listening to Mr. Vincenzo, the algebra teacher, define the word equation, when a white 1950 Ford pickup truck pulled up on the lawn outside the classroom window. A guy I recognized immediately as Big Arv Nielsen jumped out of the driver's side, leaving the motor running. There was a hole in the truck's muffler so the rumble of the engine was deafening—the belches and bops of the souped-up V-6 invaded the open classroom windows as dramatically as, thirty seconds later, Big Arv came tearing through the door the same way Herman Mooth had done in Miss Lawson's room at Clinton School four years before.

Big Arv, a heavyset, six-foot-tall Swedish kid—his full name was Arvid, but nobody called him that—was three years older than I. He'd gone to Clinton, too, and I remembered him there hanging out with another blond, crew-cut kid named Oscar Fomento who got thrown out of grammar school for setting a teacher's dress on fire. Oscar later did a spin at Bridewell for beating up his parents with a bowling pin. Big Arv wore black Chippewa motorcycle boots and kept his flat top with fenders even in the winter, never even wearing ear muffs, let alone a hat. Arv was never mean to the younger kids, though, the way his buddy Oscar Fomento had been, so I'd always thought well of him. I mean, he *could* have been mean if he'd wanted to. But he charged into the room and began choking Mr. Vincenzo, shoving him up against the blackboard. Vincenzo was taller than Arv Nielsen by three or four inches, and he was an athletic-looking thirty-year-old, but Big Arv was much more powerful and he held the algebra teacher up with one hand around the throat while he took a piece of paper out of his back pocket.

"You flunked me, Vincenzo!" Big Arv shouted, and he began slapping Vincenzo across the face with the piece of paper. "You flunked me in summer school," he yelled, "and now I can't come back here! I'll really get you for this, spaghetti head!" Then Arv released him and Vincenzo slumped to the floor. Big Arv sneered at the fallen man and spat on him. He crumpled the piece of paper, which must have been Nielsen's notice from the school that he'd flunked out, and tossed it down at Vincenzo. Big Arv looked around the classroom for a moment. All of the kids were frozen in their seats. He stared for a second directly at me in the front row, then he curled his lip, smoothed down the greased back sides of his head, and bolted out the door as fast as he'd entered. All of the kids ran to the windows and watched Big Arv clomp across the lawn in his boots, climb into the percolating pickup truck, jam it into low and zoom off, tearing long divots in the grass. We looked back at Vincenzo. He got up off the floor slowly, shook himself like a wet dog, and then ran out of the room.

I never did see Big Arv Nielsen after that day, but twenty years later a friend of mine from the old neighborhood mentioned to me that he'd heard Arv was living in Japan on the proceeds of an investment he'd made in a Broadway musical. Big Arv was apparently a wealthy man, doing just fine despite his adolescent difficulties with algebra.

My third most memorable event was not as traumatic as the run-in with Mr. Mooth or as entertaining as Big Arv Nielsen's attack on Mr. Vincenzo, but just as unforgettable. After classes let out that first day of high school, I attempted to help my friend Eddie in a fight he was having with three guys in front of school. I grabbed the shoulder of one of the boys and pulled him off, but just as I did one of Eddie's feet kicked up and he hit me smack in the nose with the heel of his boot. Blood sprayed out all over the place. It felt like my nose had exploded—it was broken. To this day I carry a bump on the bridge of my nose from that fight.

Sometimes I try to be fair-minded about school, to place these and other events in proper perspective. Could these early school years really have been as ridiculous and absurd—and painful—as I remember them? Any school kid could answer that.

The Deep Blue See

When I was in the eighth grade I was given the job of being one
of the two outdoor messengers of Clinton School. Since I was far
from being among the best-behaved students, I could only surmise
that some farsighted teacher (of whom there were very few) realized that I was well suited for that certain responsibility, that
perhaps some of my excess energy might be put to use and I'd be
honored and even eventually behave better because of this show
of faith in my ability to run errands during school hours. Either
that or they were just glad to get rid of me for a half-hour or so.

I thought it was great just because it occasionally allowed me
to get out of not only the classroom but the school. Escorting sick
kids home was the most common duty but my favorite was walking the blind piano tuner across California Avenue to and from the
bus stop.

For two weeks out of the year the old blind piano tuner used to
come each day and tune all of the pianos in the school. My job
during that time was to be at the bus stop at eight forty-five every
morning to pick him up, and then, at whatever time in the afternoon he was ready to leave, to walk him back across, wait with
him until the bus arrived, and help him board.

I became quite friendly over the two-week period that I assisted
him. I was twelve years old and the piano tuner looked to me like
any ordinary old guy with white hair in a frayed black overcoat,

except he was blind and carried a cane. My dad and I had seen Van Johnson as a blind man in the movie *Twenty-Three Paces to Baker Street*. Van Johnson had reduced an intruder to blindness by blanketing the windows and putting out the lights, trapping him—or her, as it turned out—until the cops came, but I'd never known anybody who was blind before.

I couldn't really imagine not being able to see and on the last day I asked the piano tuner if he could see anything at all. We were crossing the street and he looked up and said, "Oh yes, I see the blue. I can see the deep blue in the sky and the shadows of grey around the blue."

It was a bright sunny winter day and the sky was clear and very blue. I told him how blue it was, I didn't see any grey, and there were hardly any clouds. We were across the street and I could see the bus stopping a block away.

"Were you ever able to see?" I asked.

"Oh yes, shapes," he said. "I can see them move."

Then the bus came and I helped him up the steps and told the bus driver the old man was blind and to please wait until I'd helped him to a seat. After the piano tuner was seated I said good-bye, gave the token to the driver and got off.

While I was waiting at the corner for the traffic to slow so that I could cross, I closed my eyes and tried to imagine what it was like to be blind. I looked up with my eyes closed. I couldn't see anything. I opened them up and ran across the street.

My Mother's People

My father was Jewish, he died when I was twelve, and soon after the funeral my mother—she and my father had been divorced since I was five—was approached by my father's family who told her that the least she could do was to have me bar-mitzvahed. "For Rudolph's sake," Esther, my father's sister, said. "He would have wanted his son to be bar-mitzvahed."

She knew as well as I and my mother that Rudolph had not been at all religious. In fact, he had almost been ostracized by his family for marrying my mother, a Catholic. The marriage had not worked out because of family interference, mainly by my mother's mother, who didn't want her twenty-two-year-old daughter (my father was fifteen years older) running around with gangsters.

That part of it was true. My father ran an all-night liquor store on the corner of Chicago and Rush, next door to the Club Alabam where I used to watch the show girls rehearse on Saturday afternoons. I often ate breakfast at the small lunch counter in the store, dunking doughnuts with the organ-grinder's monkey. Big red-headed Louise ran the counter and fed me milk shakes while I waited for my dad. The place was a drop joint for stolen goods, dope, whatever somebody wanted to stash for a while. The story was that you could get anything at the store day or night. I used to see my dad giving guys penicillin shots in the basement, and I remember my mother throwing a fit when I was four years old sitting at three in the morning on a bundle of newspapers playing with a gun Bill Moore, a private cop, had given me to look at.

This kind of thing spooked my mother. My dad wore black shirts and gold ties, spoke with "dese" and "dose" and was famous for knocking guys through plate-glass windows. He'd done it twice—once in the newspaper the next day he'd been described as "that well-known man-about-town." Al Capone's brother, who was then using the name White, would come into the store often, as well as movie star Dorothy Lamour, ex-middleweight champ Tony Zale (who had a restaurant across the street—he used to show me the gloves from his matches), and whoever else was in town. We lived on Chestnut Street, next to the lake, in the Seneca Hotel, which was later described to me as containing "the lobby of the men with no last names."

My grandmother's fears were not unfounded. At one point, while my mother and father were vacationing in Hawaii, my dad received a phone call telling him somebody had been shot and that it would be best for them to extend their holiday. That was the first six-month absence of which I was aware. Later my parents spent a few months as the guest of Johnny Reata in Jamaica during another cooling-off period. Reata, my mother told me, had made his money running guns to Trujillo in the Dominican Republic.

While my mother, being a former University of Texas beauty queen, enjoyed the high-life aspects of being married to my father, the hoodlum end of it, plus the great influence her mother had over her, forced her to leave him, and I moved with her to the far North Side of the city. I continued to see my dad regularly until he died, and at no time did he ever so much as point out to me what a synagogue looked like, let alone tell me that he wanted me to be bar-mitzvahed.

For some reason my mother allowed herself to be influenced by my Aunt Esther and my dad's brother Bruno, both of whom were hypocritical Jews. Neither they, nor my Uncle Joel, Esther's husband, who also interceded on my deceased father's behalf, and who once told me, looking me straight in the eye, that deep down inside 95 percent of the Gentiles hate the Jews and could not be trusted—including me, he meant, because of my mother—went to the synagogue except for High Holiday services; social appearances. They were stingy, mean, conniving people who had always been envious of my mother's good looks and power over my father, resenting the fact that my father had ever married her.

What made it so important that I be bar-mitzvahed, they told my mother, was that I was the first son in the family. Both Bruno and Esther had had two girls apiece. I was the first one eligible to carry on the family name and tradition. And my father's father, the old man, my grandfather Ezra, who used to run numbers from his candy stand under the Addison Street el, was still alive. For his sake, before he passed away, they whined to my mother, I should be bar-mitzvahed.

So my mother was persuaded. Her mother had died a few years before so there was no one to whom she could go for advice. I had to take Hebrew lessons. Three days a week after school I would sit with a little man who smelled of smoked fish, who spoke almost no English, and memorize words I did not understand. I also went to the synagogue each Saturday morning for nearly a year after my father died to say a prayer for him. My father's family insisted that I go, even though I had never been inside a synagogue before in my life. This was necessary, it was a son's duty, they explained, and my mother reluctantly acceded to their wishes. So on Saturdays I stood at the back of the temple, put on a black skullcap and recited a prayer written in English next to the Hebrew on a little pink card.

As the bar-mitzvah day came closer I thought more and more about it, about why I was having to do this. Several times I told my mother I wouldn't go to Hebrew lessons anymore. None of it made sense to me, it was stupid, the whole thing was ridiculous. She knew I was right, but she told me to go through with it. "For your father's sake," she said. "My father's dead," I told her. "It doesn't matter to him and it wouldn't matter to him if he were alive."

But she said to finish it, then the debt to the family would be paid. This reasoning escaped me—I didn't see what we owed to them in the first place. But I stuck it out, and vowed that it really would be the end of it, that no one would ever make me do anything again.

After the bar-mitzvah, which ritual I performed like an automaton, mouthing the lines as if I weren't really there, weren't the one doing it at all, I did not see a member of my father's family—except briefly when my grandfather died—for seven years.

Passing through town those seven years later I went to see my dad's brother. Like my father, Uncle Bruno was a strong-willed, stubborn man. He had done well financially and kept his large brown brick house locked up like a fortress. When he saw me through the front-door window he motioned for me to come around the back way. "Too many bolts to undo in the front," he explained, as he and his wife admitted me through the rear entrance. They expressed their surprise at my being there, they hadn't recognized me right away. I told them I'd just come by to say hello, that was all.

Uncle Bruno insisted that I eat with them, they were just sitting down to dinner, which I did, and tell them what I'd been doing the past few years. I gave them a brief history after which Uncle Bruno asked me if I'd come to see him about a job, or did I need money?

"I don't need any money," I told him, "and I have a job. I'm a writer," I said. My uncle looked annoyed and got up and walked into the living room and sat down. I followed him in and stood by the window. "Why did you come here then, if you don't need any money?" he asked. "Out of curiosity," I said. Bruno lit a cigar. "Curious about what?" he said.

"Do you think things would have been different with me had my father lived?" I asked. "Of course they would," Bruno said. "You would have been a doctor or a lawyer or a pharmacist. Something important."

I knew it bothered Uncle Bruno that I didn't want any money, or anything else, from him. It would have bothered him had I asked for something but at least then he would have had the satisfaction of being right.

"Then I'm glad he died when he did," I said, "before we had any trouble about it."

"Being a Jew means nothing to you, does it?" said Uncle Bruno. "You're one of your mother's people."

I realized I had no reason to be there, that I should never have come. I put on my jacket.

"What did you expect?" I said, and left.

A Long Day's Night in the Naked City

My dad had a friend in New York named Edgar Volpe whom I used to visit every so often when I was in town. He died about ten years ago but until then Edgar hung out at the Villa Luna restaurant on Grand Street between Mott and Elizabeth in Little Italy. I could usually find him there in a booth at the back talking to a couple of guys who looked like they were in a hurry. Edgar was a fat man, he weighed about two hundred and fifty pounds and stood maybe five-foot-eight with his shoes on. He always looked like he had plenty of time to talk.

From what little Edgar told me about his relationship with my dad I gathered that they had collaborated on a few liquor heists during the thirties. Edgar never really opened up to me and there was no reason that he should have. He was always very nice and insisted on buying me lunch at the Villa. One afternoon when I was eating linguini with clam sauce and discussing with Edgar the vicissitudes of the New York Rangers, of whom he was an avid follower, a short, wiry guy came in and over to our table and held out to Edgar an envelope. "It's there," he said. "I'm fuckin' t'rough wid it."

Edgar didn't touch the envelope, motioning with a nod for the man to lay it on the table, which he did. "Siddown, why doncha," said Edgar. "Have some linguini." "Nah, t'anks," said the man. "I got my cab outside. I'm workin'." He shifted from foot to foot and looked quickly around the restaurant. The man was about thirty-five to forty, five-nine or ten. He was wearing sunglasses so I couldn't see his eyes. "So we're t'rough now, right?" he said to Edgar. "Dis makes it." Edgar nodded slowly and gave the man a small half-smile. "If you say so," said Edgar. "I'm always around if you want." The wiry man gave a loud, short laugh. "I hope to fuck I won't," he said. He looked around again and back at Edgar, then at me, then back at Edgar. "So I'm goin'," he said. "And t'anks, Mr. Volpe. T'anks a million." "Anytime," said Edgar.

The man left and Edgar slowly picked up the envelope and put it into his inside jacket pocket. "Funny guy," Edgar said to me. "He was a cop. Then he's moonlightin' one night guardin' some buildin's over onna West Side an' almost gets his eye shot out. Some fancy lookin' white broad is out stoppin' cars—Mercedes, Cadillacs, Jags, expensive models—an' tellin' the driver she got a flat tire or somethin'. Then as the driver's about to give her a lift, a black guy dressed like a bum comes up behind the broad and drags her into an alley. Naturally, the driver jumps out and chases the attacker. I mean this broad is a doll, dressed to the nines, a real fox, an' the guy thinks he's got somethin', see, so he goes to help her, right? The black guy takes off when he sees the driver comin' and drops the broad. The driver comforts the broad, takes her into his car. Asks her where she wants to go. She puts a gun to his head, opens the door and the black guy gets in the back, also wid a gun. They're workin' together, right? They rob the driver and have him drive to his house or apartment, which they clean out the jewels and cash. Nice scam. Worked thirty-two times inna row until my pal there, the cop who's moonlightin' in order to save money for his weddin', spots this couple in the act.

"Sonny there, the cop, tries to pull the black guy outta this Mercedes, an' the broad shoots him inna head. Sonny's lyin' onna ground next to the car and the black guy falls out right onna

Sonny. Sonny's bleedin' like crazy but figures if he's gonna die he's not goin' down alone, so he plugs the nigger, passes out.

"When he wakes up, Sonny's inna hospital wid his eye bandaged. He's alive an' the doctors tell 'im a couple operations an' maybe he won' hafta lose his right eye. The nigger's dead; the broad got away clean. While he's inna hospital, the broad Sonny's engaged to never even comes to see him. She thinks he's gonna die anyway, right? He'd already given her, what, maybe ten, fourteen t'ousand dollars for the wedding. She's why he's fuckin' moonlightin' inna first place. So while he's inna hospital fightin' for his life she runs off wid some other guy. By the time Sonny gets out he's in deep shit 'cause the Police Department insurance policy won't cover him since he was off duty an' workin' for somebody else. So he needs money, he comes to me. He's suin' the insurance company, the owner of the buildin' he's guardin' that night, the cops, everybody he can think of. On top of that he's afraid to go see the broad t'rew him over 'cause he'd put six inna her. Now he's pushin' a hack tryna get back on his feet. I give him a good deal, plenya time to pay me back, right? Why not. Your dad, he helped out plenya guys."

No More Mr. Nice Guy

My buddy Magic Frank lived next door to me in Chicago with his two older brothers, Woody and Jerry, and their mother. I spent quite a bit of time at their house from the age of ten until I was seventeen, and there were few dull moments. The brothers were constantly hammering on one another and their mother regularly pounded on them. All three boys were bruisers. Mealtime at their house was like a scene out of the movie *One Million B.C.*, in which the cavemen wrestled each other and tore each other's lungs out just to snatch a piece of meat.

The biggest and toughest of the three was the eldest, Jerry, also known as Moose. Moose was a legendary Chicago athlete who had starred in basketball and football in high school and then went on to play tackle and guard at two or three different universities. After the boys' father died, Moose came home and took over the family automobile insurance business, which was failing. Moose decided to specialize in insuring so-called uninsurable motorists, drivers who had been in multiple accidents or had acquired so many moving-violation citations that the more regular companies felt they were too poor a risk. The rates Moose charged these people were exorbitant but if they failed to pay on time Moose attached their property, usually their car, until they came across. If their collateral was insufficient, there would be other, less benign consequences.

Moose's first partner in this enterprise was a six-foot-tall, three-hundred-pound monster named Cueball Bluestein. Moose was six-three and two-twenty, so they comprised quite a tag team. Cueball was the designated enforcer, although Moose was no slouch if push came to shove came to pull some deadbeat's ear off and mail it to his wife and kids. The boys at Mid-Nite Insurance knew how to do business in Chicago.

Cueball really was a beast, though. Whenever he saw me or Frankie he'd hit us so hard on the arm or shoulder we'd carry the bruises for three weeks. The worst thing was to get caught in a narrow hallway with him where he'd ram his bulk into you against a wall, squeezing out all of your breath, then leave you gasping on the floor while he waddled away, laughing. I hated him, and so did Frank.

After I left the neighborhood I kept in touch with Frankie, and through him I heard news of his brothers but I didn't know much about what had become of Cueball Bluestein, other than that at some point he'd been confined to Clark County, Nevada—which includes Las Vegas—as part of some kind of Mafia deal. I knew Cueball was a big gambler and that he'd become a hit man for the Chicago mob, but I didn't know any of the details until I had dinner with Frank one night in Chicago years later.

According to Frank, after Cueball and Moose parted company in the insurance business—though they remained friends—Cueball went to work for Dodo Saltimbocca, the Chicago crime boss. The night before Saltimbocca was scheduled to testify in front of a commission investigating organized crime, Cueball, who was as close to Saltimbocca as you could get, being his aide and confidant, shot and killed him. The other Chicago bosses thought that Saltimbocca was going to rat on them so they got Cueball to pull the trigger. For this good deed Cueball was sent to Vegas and installed as the number two man under Sammy Eufemia, for whom he labored a number of years. The Chicago mob ruled Vegas and the New York mob ruled Atlantic City and all was, if not entirely copacetic, understood.

The Chicago cops, as well as the Feds, knew that Cueball had murdered Saltimbocca, but the deal was that they wouldn't touch him as long as he remained in Clark County. All went swimmingly until Sammy Eufemia wound up piled on top of his brother, Bitsy, in a shallow grave in an Indiana cornfield. Both Bitsy and Sammy had been shot in the exact same spot in the back of their heads. Dodo Saltimbocca had been similarly executed.

Had Cueball made the move in order to become number one in Vegas? Or was it a play on the part of the New York crowd looking to horn in on forbidden territory? Frankie didn't know, he told me, and didn't want to. He did know that Cueball was currently in prison in Nevada on a ten-year rap for receiving stolen property, mostly jewelry. On his income tax form each year, Frank said, Cueball always listed his profession as "jeweler."

"He was never a nice guy," I said to Frank.

"True," Frankie said, "but he was from the neighborhood, same as us. Also same as us," said Frank, "his father died when he was young. I'm sure that's one of the reasons I got into as many fights as I did when I was a kid. I was upset."

"Maybe," I said, "but you didn't become a killer, and neither did I."

"Well," said Frank, "probably Cueball was more pissed off about it than we were."

Uncle Buck

I've always loved my Uncle Buck, my mother's brother, and after speaking to him on the telephone recently it occurred to me just how important a person he's always been to me; how I've always looked to him for an example of how I should live my life, especially in my father's absence.

As a teenager Buck rode an Indian motorcycle and did daredevil stunts at carnivals and fairs. In college—Georgia Tech—he captained the fencing team and was the Georgia state amateur golfing champion. After graduating with two engineering degrees, Buck went off to help build the railroad through the Yukon. He constructed bridges in Ireland, Portugal and Burma, lumber-jacked on Iron Mountain in Michigan and during the war was in the Seabees as well as an operative in the OSS, winding up with the rank of full Commander in the Navy.

Since my mother's been married four times and my father died young, I suppose it was only natural that I'd fix on Uncle Buck as my most stable paternal figure. Physically, Buck has always been an impressive man: at seventy years old he still looks like a cross between Errol Flynn and Douglas Fairbanks, Senior. He lived with us on and off while I was a kid so I was able to spend a considerable amount of time with him. As a disciplinarian he was consistent and never unreasonable: if you did something wrong and didn't own up to it or whined about how rough or unfair things were, he took off his belt and used it. In that respect he was like the Ghurkas, the Nepalese soldiers who, once having removed their knives from their scabbards, even to clean them, could not replace them without drawing blood. Once Uncle Buck was pushed to the point of having taken off his belt, you knew nothing you might say or do short of running out and never coming back was going to prevent him from giving you a swipe or two across the rear. I'm convinced now that the actual physical punishment was not nearly so damaging as the psychological anguish caused by the sight of Uncle Buck beginning to unbuckle his belt.

Buck has always been quite a ladies' man. He can talk with ease to any woman and charm her. I actually used to more than half enjoy watching him "steal" my girlfriends away from me when I was fifteen and sixteen by his smile and engaging manner. I was always a willing student in Uncle Buck's school of How to Win and Influence Young Ladies though I could never hope to outdo the master.

Uncle Buck's first marriage, however, lasted only six years and ended badly: his wife found him with another woman and she divorced him. That marriage produced one son, my cousin Carl. Buck's second and last, to this point, official union lasted four years and ended even more rudely: he caught his wife with another man and divorced her. That marriage produced one daughter, my cousin Christine. Buck's relationships with his children, both of whom were raised primarily by their mothers, have not been very successful. He demands a great deal of them, expecting them to be as independently minded and variously accomplished as he is and it has caused difficulties. Since I'm one step removed, a nephew, not a son or daughter, his attitude towards me has been more relaxed. We're friends as well as uncle and nephew, and there has been less pressure exerted by him on me to live up to any particular standards. When I finished high school he offered to help get me into the United States Naval Academy at Annapolis, and when I declined he didn't push the matter, even though I knew he would have liked me to have gone there. For some reason, he told me not too long ago, he's always had confidence in my ability to get along; he trusts me, as I do him. That seems to be the most important component of our relationship.

When I was twelve years old Buck moved to Tampa, Florida, and became a housing tract builder. I drove from Chicago that summer with my cousin Carl to visit him, and we were immediately put to work on a construction job. My uncle recently moved his office from the one he occupied in Tampa for twenty-five years. It's difficult for me to picture him in an office without the Atlantic sailfish he caught in 1952 on the wall over his head behind the desk, and the dusty, blue-backed copies of *Dutton's Navigation and Piloting* and *Advanced Celestial Navigation* on the shelf beside him.

Buck put my cousin and me to work in the desert north of town, a wasteland soon to be covered with cracker-box houses for the rapidly expanding population. The heat was unbearable: in the morning, when it was eighty-two degrees at eight o'clock, I felt beaten, trapped. There seemed to be no sky, only a hovering holocaust. I remember the foreman on the first job I worked for my uncle, a completely bald and eyebrowless man named Snood. He looked like a hairless gorilla.

The first day Snood drove me in his pickup truck out to the middle of nowhere and stopped, signalling me to get out and follow him. We walked over a rise in the sand until we came to a deep, narrow pit where a group of men were fitting together enormous sections of sewer pipe.

"This is a new boy," Snood yelled down to them. "He'll help you this morning." Snood then turned abruptly back to the truck, climbed in and was gone. I looked back down at the men, none of whom seemed to take the slightest interest in me. I slid down the sandy slope into the ditch. Two of the men were struggling to keep a piece of pipe in place while four others attempted to attach another piece to it. I helped the men steady the section. When it was done, one of the men said to me, "I'm in for rape, how about you?"

All of the men laughed except one, the only black man on the job, who was digging shovelsful of sand out of the ditch and tossing them up over the edge.

"As you can see," said another of the men, "we poor peed-a-beds is tryin' to lay this cocksuckin' pipe in this goddamn ditch so some sonofabitchin' whore's ass can have hot water runnin' out her kitchen sink with a turn o' the same lily white wrist works her old man's joint. Ain't nothin' to it so long as you're as stupid and fucked up as the rest of us."

We worked for an hour or so before one of the men told me I could go take a drink if I wanted to. I climbed out of the ditch up to where an inverted trash can with a spigot sat on top of a card table under two of the skinniest and least shade-providing trees around. Next to the water can were two plastic cups, one red and one black. I filled the red one and drank it all in one gulp. Then I remembered my uncle's admonition about not drinking much water when you're hot and tired and short of breath so I only swallowed a small amount of a second cup, gargled the rest, and spit it out. Then I scrambled down into the ditch and went back to work.

"How come there are just two cups up there?" I asked one of the men.

"The red one's for the nigger," he said.

During the lunch break I lay down under the two skinny trees. At twelve-thirty Snood drove up and shouted to me to come over and hop into his truck, which I did. He drove me to another desert area but one within sight of a few houses. He drove slowly along a levelled stretch of yellow-green dirt.

"See that shit piled on the sides of the curbs?" he said. "That's lime rock." He stopped the truck and looked over at me. "Grab the shovel off the back and start shovellin' it off the curbs back into the street. We've got to shoot it tomorrow."

I got out and removed the shovel from the rear and watched Snood drive away. I looked around for a while then walked over to the curb and began shovelling. I had shovelled the lime rock completely off of one curb and had just begun working on the other when a steamroller came up the road, flattening the surface and forcing the excess lime rock back up onto the curb I had shovelled clean. The driver, I later learned, was a former Alabama sheriff who had spent ten years in the slam for child molesting. He smiled as he went by and off down another newly begun road. I just stood there and stared at the lime rock covering the curb. It was a little disheartening so I went and sat down under a tree, one that was a bit more shade-providing than the ones where we had been laying sewer pipe, and fell asleep. By the time Snood returned I was awake and I ran over to the pickup, threw the shovel in the back and got in. Snood didn't even look at the curbs. "Almost forgot about you," he chuckled.

My uncle would always show up at the job site in his banged-up Cadillac convertible, which he used like a pickup truck. He'd jump down into a ditch and show everybody how to dig or hop up on a roof and demonstrate the proper way to set trusses as if nobody else had ever dug a ditch or set a truss before. Inevitably, as he was trying to drive away, Buck's car would get stuck in the mud or sand. He would scramble around in his trunk for tools or boards and the workers would have to help push him out. The amazing thing to me was that despite all of Buck's eccentricities and often unreasonable demands people enjoyed working for him. He was obviously slightly insane but his spirit was ingenuous.

Shortly after the revolution in Cuba, Buck took Pops, my grandfather, with him to see what the situation was like. While walking through a plaza in Havana a squad of Fidelistas surrounded them and arrested my uncle. At their headquarters they showed Buck a photograph of a general of Batista's for whom he was a dead—almost literally so—ringer. The only reason they hadn't shot him in the street was that they couldn't understand what he'd be doing walking along in broad daylight in the company of an old man. The general's picture was on the front page of that day's newspaper. The resemblance between the general and my uncle was indeed remarkable, and after he'd proven his identity Buck bought a dozen copies of the paper to take home. Pops told me that Buck also did some magic tricks for the soldiers and they gave him a box of Upmann cigars, supposedly Castro's favorite brand.

When I was eighteen years old and travelling through Europe, I went into the Traveler's Aid office in the railroad station at Ghent, Belgium, to find out how to get to Zeveneken, the nearby town where a friend of mine lived. A man in the office who'd come in to check a train schedule told me he'd show me where to catch the bus and led me outside to the front of the station. He spoke English and showed me on the post at the stop that the next bus for Zeveneken was not due to leave for almost four hours. He said that his wife and child were due in at about the same time on a train from Antwerp. He looked me over carefully and asked if I was hungry. I told him I was. "Come on then," he said. "You can come home with me for a while and we will eat. Then I will drive you back here."

I was very hungry and decided to go along. He was a small

man, in his forties, pasty-faced but with very dark eyes and hair. He spoke English with a strange accent, definitely not French or Flemish. "You're not from Belgium originally," I asked him, "are you?"

We were in his *deux chevaux*, trundling down a cobblestone street. Ghent looked to me like a storybook land. Even the rain had stopped, leaving everything glistening, immaculate. I was glad to be out of Paris.

"I am Russian, from Minsk," said my benefactor. "My name is Bulgakov." "Did you learn English in Russia?" I asked. "You speak perfectly." "I lived in the United States for fourteen years," he said. "I was a navigator on boats, first in the Gulf of Mexico, then on the Great Lakes. I lived for two years in Galveston, Texas, then for twelve years outside Chicago."

"I grew up partially in Chicago," I told Bulgakov. "Where did you live there?" "In Skokie," he said. "On Laramie Street." I laughed. "Really?" I said. "My Uncle Buck lived for many years on Laramie Street in Skokie. He was in the construction business and built most of the houses in that part of town."

Bulgakov looked at me and half-smiled. "Colby Construction Company, yes? Your uncle was Buck Colby?" "Yes!" I said. "Were you a neighbor of his? I used to spend a lot of time there." "My father and I bought a house from your uncle," said Bulgakov. "He was a good fellow. It was a good house." "That's amazing," I said. "Does your father still live there?" "No," said Bulgakov, "he is dead." "What a coincidence, though," I said, "your knowing my Uncle Buck." I introduced myself and we shook hands as he drove. "Why did you come here?" I asked. "Are you still a navigator?" "No, I don't work on boats now. I am a stateless person, allowed to remain because my wife and son are Belgian citizens. My wife works and I take care of the boy and the house. Also, I am writing a book about what happened to me in America."

I was, of course, about to ask what had happened to him in America when Bulgakov pulled the car into the driveway of a modest but handsome two-story house on a short street. "This is a nice place," I said as we got out of the car. Bulgakov again gave me a half smile. "We'll go in," he said. "I'll make you some dinner and I will tell you a story about your country." As I ate, or attempted to eat (there was too much for me) the wonderful meal Bulgakov prepared—steak, spinach, potatoes, salad, bread, cake—he told me how during the fifties, because he was Russian, he had been blacklisted as a Communist and prevented from working on ships in the United States.

"I was *not* a Communist," he said. "It was because of Stalin that my father and I left the Soviet Union and went to America. My mother and sister were murdered by the pig Stalin. America was *freedom*! We were good citizens. My father could not speak English, only a little. He was too old to learn, but I became a citizen, I studied hard, and then the government says I am a spy and I cannot work."

"Did they prosecute you?" I asked. "As a spy, I mean." "No. They *per*secuted me, made sure I could not get a job on a seagoing vessel anywhere in the country. The unions would do nothing for me, pretended I was dead. So much for the so-called 'commie' unions! Look, I'll show you something." Bulgakov went upstairs and returned a few minutes later, carrying a large box.

"These are the letters," Bulgakov said, pulling papers from the box. "Letters and documents from the ten years I spent clearing my name. I spent ten thousand dollars in legal fees to prove that I was not a Communist, to make the government allow me to work again on boats, to remove my name from the blacklist. It took all those years and all that money to accomplish this. My father died, not only from old age but shame and pain, knowing the accusations were false. We had to sell the house your uncle built so that we could have money to live. Nobody would hire me. I was a 'security risk.' Such shit it was. Finally I did it, I cleared my name, and when I did I left America and came here, first to Brussels, where I knew some people, then, after I married, to Ghent. I gave up my American passport, renounced my citizenship that I had studied so hard to earn. I am a free citizen now. I live here, I hope I will die here. Do you want more coffee?"

"No, no thank you," I said. "I can't eat anymore. That's a terrible story." "Yes, terrible," said Bulgakov. "But there are many worse stories, of course. Especially in the Soviet Union. That is the only place worse than the United States."

Bulgakov drove me back to the train station where I met his wife, a pretty redhaired woman, and their two-year-old son. He told his wife that I was a "stray" from the USA, that he'd given me a meal and allowed me to freshen up at their house. I felt better not only for having eaten but Bulgakov had also insisted that I take a bath and shave. I was extremely grateful for the hospitality, I told his wife, and would be glad to return the same if they came to America.

"Thank you but no," said Bulgakov, not smiling as he spoke. "My wife and son don't need that other kind of hospitality I was so privileged to receive, the kind that is beyond your control." We took his wife and son to the car and then Bulgakov walked me to the bus stop. "So good-bye, my friend," Bulgakov said, shaking my hand. "Please do not thank me anymore. I want you to know I loved the United States, I loved my house your uncle built, it was a fine house. I am sorry but I will never see it again. I don't *have* to stay here. I *want* to. I am a free man. Good-bye."

We shook hands and Bulgakov walked back to his car. The bus to Zeveneken arrived and I got on. I took a window seat and looked back for Bulgakov. He was holding up his son and talking to him.

When I told my uncle about meeting Bulgakov, Buck remembered him, and he recalled that he'd actually sold the house to the elder Bulgakov. Buck knew that the son had had some difficulty with the government, but he thought it had been with the immigration service. My uncle didn't know the extent of Bulgakov's problem, however, and didn't know why he'd sold the house.

My main pastime with Uncle Buck has been fishing. He's always had a boat for us to go out on in the Gulf of Mexico and we've spent most of our time together that way. No expedition was a success, however—at least in Buck's estimation—unless there was an element of real danger involved. Buck and his second wife had almost been killed during a race across Lake Michigan when they were caught in a storm and the mast of Buck's sailboat broke in two, and in February of 1973 my uncle and I were almost killed aboard a boat we were sailing for a friend of his across the Gulf Stream from Nassau to Coral Gables when a vicious squall came within a few feet of cracking us up on a breakwater off Miami. Before we left on that trip from the Bahamas I asked Uncle Buck when we'd be back in Tampa. "Who knows?" he said. "We may never get back."

Once when I was about fourteen we ran aground on a sandbar several miles out in the Gulf. Rather than wait the thirty minutes or so until the tide was due to change, Buck told me to get out of the boat and push. I dutifully jumped over the side and had begun to rock the boat in order to free it when I spotted a large dorsal fin heading straight for me. I immediately hoisted myself back into the boat and watched the fin glide by. "What are you doing?" asked my uncle. "Why aren't you in the water?" "Shark," I told him. "A big one just swam by." "Don't worry about the sharks," he said. "I'll tell you if I see one."

The last time Buck was in East Africa he packed himself a

lunch one day and wandered off into the bush alone. At some point during his hike he was confronted on the trail by a large native who refused to or could not speak either English or Swahili, in which languages my uncle attempted to ingratiate himself. "He was a mean-looking guy and was carrying a big machete," Buck told me. "He wouldn't let me by." "What did you do?" I asked. "Turn around and go back?" "No," Buck laughed, "Of course not. I had a wonderful day; I walked for miles and saw all kinds of wild game." "What about the native?" I said. "How did you get past him?" "Oh, no problem," said Buck. "I just gave him my lunch."

In recent years Buck has developed a particular fondness for exceedingly primitive places. Now seventy years old, he's spent the greater part of the last few building a house, his "last resort" as he calls it, on the island of Utila, off the coast of Honduras directly north of La Ceiba and east of Monkey-River Town, Belize. The local population numbers approximately three thousand. There are power poles along the one main road of the island but as of yet no electrical lines. Power is provided several hours a day by generator. Most of the inhabitants are descendants of pirates; the most common surnames are Morgan and Jones. It is a remittance island: since there is no industry all of the young adults leave as soon as they are able in order to find work, sending money home to relatives still on Utila. The waters around the island are shark-infested but the fishing is excellent. Gambling is legal in Honduras and there is an island bar where men and women play roulette and shoot craps in their bare feet while hens and roosters strut around among their legs on the floor. Prostitution is practiced openly. There is a town maniac, a sorcerer of whom everyone is afraid; every so often he has a fit and jumps around in the street shouting and screeching and threatening passersby with the evil eye. The feeling is of a frontier outpost, a barely civilized settlement where anything can happen, much as in the novels of Gabriel García Márquez, who writes of his nearby homeland, Colombia.

The big news these days in Honduras—as it is everywhere in Central America—is the revolution; the vying of the two government parties, the Reds and the Blues, both military groups who are presently fighting for the right to govern the country. Counter-insurgency groups are training in the mountains of mainland Honduras, from which they make forays into Guatemala to combat the Cuban-backed rebels. In the capital, Tegucigalpa, called "Tuh-goosey," dozens of left-wing soldiers have been abducted by masked gunmen, ostensibly secret police similar to Papa Doc's Tontons Macoute in Haiti. Former members of the ousted Nicaraguan National Guard and Salvadoran police on loan have set up death squads in order to frighten the liberals; however, the Lorenzo Zelaya Popular Revolutionary Command, a left-wing guerilla group, recently claimed credit for the shooting of two United States military advisers and the bombing of the Honduran Congress, marking, in their words, the start of an "armed struggle against the Yankee imperialism."

The people of Utila, the treasure hunters, impoverished fishermen, cayman-skinners and others, cannot help but wonder what will happen to them if there is a successful revolution. Their island is isolated, with little to offer any government other than a location for a military outpost. Uncle Buck has built his house on a needle-tip peninsula, a strip of sand accessible by foot only at low tide. It's a beautiful structure, a roundhouse with twelve exterior doors and an exposed wood beam ceiling. Concrete posts sunk twelve feet below the high tide line support the house, making it the most well-built edifice on the island. I told my uncle that when the rebels take control they're going to make his house their command post on the island. "How many years do you think it'll be before they take over?" Buck asked me. "Four, five, tops," I said. "Well, that's all right," he said. "They can have it after that. I don't think I'll be much good to anybody after I'm seventy-five anyway."

Most of the island is still jungle and swamp; for transportation Buck rides around on a large Kawasaki motorcycle, and has rapidly become a well-known figure to the local citizenry. One afternoon Buck spotted a group of young boys looking like Buñuel's *Los Olvidados* dragging a dead python down the main street of the town. He went over to them and asked them how much they would be willing to sell it for. They couldn't name a price so my uncle offered them fifty cents and made the deal.

Buck took the python, which was about seven or eight feet long, and with his knife proceeded to skin it on the spot. He showed the boys, who may or may not already have known, the proper way to make the initial incision, slicing the underbelly, and how to then split it into two sections, peeling back the skins carefully so as to preserve them in one still-connected piece. Severing the head proved impossible without a machete, the python's vertebra being almost as large as a man's, so after several minutes of futile hacking with the knife failed to dislodge it, Buck left the head attached. He took the severed hide and nailed it to a board, then sprinkled it liberally with salt. All of this he performed while in the middle of the main road, a large crowd having gathered around to observe the procedure. Nailed and salted, the python skin was placed on the roof of a friend's house, where it could dry unmolested.

When he was fifty Uncle Buck had skinned an alligator some cracker had shot on a pier on the Hillsborough River in Tampa. I was twelve years old then and I stood like the kids on the street in Honduras and watched him peel that gator for five hours in the sun. He let me carry the skin home, where we tacked it up on the side of the garage. I knew it was a five-hundred-dollar fine if he got caught with that alligator hide and I asked him if he worried about it being seen.

"People have to live," he said, "not worry. A man can't do both and expect to get away with anything."

When I reminded Buck, after he'd told me about the python, how I'd watched him skin the gator and what he'd said that day, he laughed and told me he'd been offered a hundred dollars for it by a county sheriff.

"He could have arrested me," said Buck, "but I just told him I couldn't let it go for less than three. Hell, it was *hot* out there on that pier."

I suppose the essence of my image of Uncle Buck is best reflected by his reaction to the disastrous tropical storm of 1975, when the worst hurricane in the history of the western hemisphere hit Central America, the hardest hit being Honduras. I hadn't heard from Uncle Buck for a while, and after reading the newspaper reports of the widespread death and destruction followed by famine and disease in his adopted republic, I was worried about him. A week after the hurricane I received a card postmarked La Ceiba. "Dear Nephew," it read. "Stories of Honduras highly exaggerated. Have seen only four dead, three bridges & roads out & killed two snakes trying to put oil in engine. Best, Uncle Buck."

Speakeasy

My actual introduction to the liquor business came not via my dad but through a guy about ten years older than I was named Arnie Farraday. Arnie was from Tupelo, Mississippi, and worked a regular job as a grave digger. His claim to fame, although it was never Arnie who spoke of it, was that he had once killed a man with one punch.

When I was first told this it seemed to me an incredible story, seeing as how Arnie was only five-foot-five-inches tall and was, as far as I could tell, an extraordinarily even-tempered person. What had indeed happened was that while Arnie was in the Army his wife had divorced him and married another man. This hurt Arnie terribly; he loved his wife very much, as well as their three-year-old daughter. One day in the barracks Arnie was showing a few of his buddies pictures of his wife and daughter when a drunken soldier stumbled in, pointed to the photograph of Arnie's ex-wife, and said, "Who's that whore?" Arnie hit him once in the face, knocking the soldier backwards across the bunk. When he fell he hit his head on the railing and died. Arnie was given a general discharge.

He and I worked together for a while delivering liquor to "colored speakeasies," as Arnie called them, in Evanston, just across the Chicago line. Evanston is a dry town, and the speaks ordered their booze from the Howard Street taverns. We once delivered a dozen cases of Scotch during a snowstorm on Christmas Eve. We had to carry the cases down a narrow gangway to the back of an old wooden house, then down a long flight of precipitous, icy steps to the door, or rather doors—there was an outside screen door, then a wooden one, then a thick, soundproof door which opened into a large, dark cellar through which Arnie and I carried the cases; then up some stairs into an enormous kitchen where several girls sat around a table in slips and housecoats playing cards.

The proprietress, a heavyset middle-aged black woman with pince-nez hanging down her bosom, thanked us, and told us where to set the cases. She gave us each a glass of eggnog generously spiked with bourbon, and smiled at us, displaying at least five shiny gold teeth on the left side of her mouth. Having been there before, Arnie kidded around with the woman, whose name was Williestine, while I watched the girls. I was sixteen and had never been in a whorehouse before. All of the girls were different shades of brown, none of them were black. I thought they were the most interesting and beautiful women I had ever seen. Williestine, however, caught me looking and snapped, "These ain't your kind, honey. These for Easter rabbits," she said. "Chocolate bunnies. You dig?"

I was embarrassed and put down my drink. Williestine laughed but I could tell that for some reason she was really annoyed with me. I stood looking out the kitchen window at the blowing white flakes while Arnie finished his eggnog and bourbon. Nat Cole was singing "The Christmas Song" on the radio. Finally Arnie grinned his handsome, little boy's face at Williestine, joked a bit more, and said good-bye, having me precede him down the stairs and out the back door.

"What was she so upset about?" I asked Arnie when we were outside.

"Oh, she was just jealous you were paying so much attention to the girls," drawled Arnie, "instead of to her. My, my," he said, and laughed, as we made our way through the snow to the car, "that Williestine sure do have her pride."

Buddies

My old friend Moe called me up this afternoon from Chicago just to say hello. I hadn't seen or talked to him for almost two years, since the last time I was in Chicago, so it was a nice surprise. Moe is an automobile mechanic, he runs his own little garage up on North Clark Street near the lake. He still looks and sounds like he did twenty years ago, like a less-sensitive, more powerfully built James Dean, the same smile and coloring, with a high-pitched, almost girlish voice. I've always thought of Moe as the kind of guy my dad would have liked, that he would have picked up right away on Moe's inherent honesty and respected his ability to get things done.

Moe helped me to buy my first motorcycle—a Triumph—and my first car, a maroon 1955 Buick Century. When I first met Moe, who is six years older than I am, he was twenty-one and had the reputation of being one of the best wheel men in the city of Chicago. He'd recently been discharged for life with a hideous circular burnlike scar on his right biceps.

Moe had been forced to join the Army after he and a buddy, Davey Floyd, had gotten drunk on moonshine in Paris, Tennessee, Davey's hometown, then broken into the Cadillac agency on Main Street, hot-wired an Eldorado and driven straight out through the showroom's plate-glass window. The cops caught them only after Moe had run three roadblocks and the Eldorado

had run out of gas. Moe had done time previously at St. Charles
Reformatory outside Chicago, as a juvenile for car theft, so when
the judge in Tennessee gave him a choice between the Army or
jail—a common practice in southern courts in the fifties—Moe
did not hesitate to choose enlistment, as did Davey.

My cousin Chris introduced me to Moe, they were friends, and
Moe immediately took me under his wing. I began hanging out
with them and their gang, all of whom were in their twenties or
older, when I was fifteen. They introduced me to motorcycles,
grain alcohol, older women and various other pastimes attractive
to a healthy, reasonably curious midwestern adolescent. One time
Moe bought a machine gun down on Maxwell Street for eighty
dollars and came by my house to show it to me. I remember my
mother calling me in for dinner while Moe and I stood on the sidewalk by the open trunk of his '57 Chrysler New Yorker as he
pieced together the tommy gun.

Not long after I graduated from high school I began traveling,
and did not return to Chicago for seven or eight years. When I
finally did I called Moe, who was working out of the garage behind his mother's house, and he told me to come right over. When
I got there Moe threw me a set of car keys, said, "Hi, man, follow
me," and motioned for me to get into a huge Cadillac convertible.
He climbed into a Ford van and drove off. I started up the Caddy
and tailed him. Moe drove up and down streets I'd never seen before, stopping about twenty minutes later in an alley. He jumped
out of the van, signalled for me to wait, and he ran through a gangway into the back of a house. In ten minutes he came out, hopped
back into the van and pulled away. I followed him for another
twenty minutes or so until he parked in front of a house on a quiet
street in Evanston. Moe went into the house and came out five
minutes later, opened the door on the driver's side of the Cadillac,
motioned for me to shove over, which I did, slid behind the wheel,

cranked the ignition, peeled away from the curb and said, "Hey, man, great to see you. Where've you been?"

Moe never explained why he'd just had me follow him all over town and I never asked. I understood that he trusted me, that was enough. If I showed that I couldn't handle it he wouldn't ask me to do anything again. I knew if that ever happened Moe wouldn't make a big deal of it, there just would never be another opportunity for me to prove myself. I knew then, too, as I know now, that if I had to I could trust Moe with my life.

Moe was always a great mechanic. He knew I was different, that my ambitions weren't the same as his, and perhaps because of that we got along well. After I began to write and my books were published, Moe made an effort to show his confidence in me that way, too, by buying the books. When I told him that I'd be happy to give him copies, he said, "No, man, you're the author. You write, the public buys. I'm the public." I appreciated this, coming from Moe, knowing that he'd read about six books in his life, all of them having to do with rebuilding automobile or airplane engines.

This afternoon on the phone Moe told me he'd been in New Jersey recently on a vacation with his girlfriend and had spotted a double-decker Greyhound Scenicruiser sitting in a yard just off the highway. It was raining that day, he said, and he pulled off the road and went over to have a look at the bus. As he was walking around looking it over a guy came out of a house and asked Moe if he could help him. Moe asked if the guy owned the bus and if it was for sale. The guy answered yes on both counts and Moe asked him how much. "Thirty-five hundred," said the guy. "Thirty-five hundred!" Moe said to me on the phone. "Jesus, I thought, the goddamn engine alone was worth more than that. It had a big Detroit diesel in there. So I gave him a thousand bucks and a bogus check for twenty-five hundred on the spot. I worked on it for a couple of days and then drove it back to Chicago. My girlfriend drove the car."

"How could you work on it," I asked Moe, "without your tools?"

"Hey, man, you know me," said Moe. "All I need is a wrench, pliers and a screwdriver and I can make anything go." He explained that he was running a shuttle service with the bus between Chicago and the Wisconsin resorts. "I'm thinking of operating my own personal service with it down to Disney World in Orlando," Moe told me.

Since I live in California now I don't often get to see Moe, but the last time I did, two years ago in Chicago, I was staying at a ritzy hotel on the Near North Side. Moe came over to see me and we had a few beers in my room before going out to dinner. When we came out of the hotel there was one of Moe's inevitable Cadillac convertibles sitting at the curb right in front. The doorman, who obviously had been going crazy trying to decide whether or not to call a tow truck for the hour and a half Moe's Cadillac had been parked there, not knowing what to do about a late-model fire engine-red Eldorado with no license plates or city sticker that might possibly belong to some Syndicate bigshot, just stared at us as we got in and drove away.

As soon as Moe had maneuvered the Cad across Michigan Avenue and onto the Outer Drive, where he could let his souped-up V-8 loose, he turned to me and said, "Life's full of problems, man, that's just the way things are. But every so often we do have some fun, don't we?" Then Moe grinned like James Dean and gave it the gun.

Big Steve, King Levinsky & Other Real Americans I Have Known

The only one of my friends who remembers my dad is Big Steve. Steve has been interested in history and current events ever since I've known him, and that's thirty years now. We grew up together in Chicago and always have been close friends. When we were about ten, the Mohawk gas station on the corner of Rockwell Street and Devon Avenue was giving away drinking glasses with pictures of all the presidents of the United States on them; underneath each president's picture were the dates of his term in office. I remember that Steve made his father buy gas at the Mohawk station just so he could get the set of six with a fill-up. Steve studied a glass at every meal, memorizing the presidents' names and dates of tenure. "John Quincy Adams," he'd say to me as we walked together to school, "1825 to 1829." A half-block farther on he'd say, "Zachary Taylor, 1849 to 1850. Died in office." And so on. That's how Big Steve learned the presidents.

Now he's an executive producer for network television news, and we saw each other when Steve came out to San Francisco to cover the 1984 Democratic National Convention. More than a few people we knew in the old days might be just a little surprised that Big Steve made good. One of them would certainly be Peter Miscinski, one of our high school history teachers. Miscinski hated Big Steve because Steve was a class clown, a joker who loved to poke fun at him. Miscinski was an easy target, though, and was hardly a match for Steve's witty and often caustic remarks. Big Steve brought a pillow with him to class one day, put it on his desk and laid his head down. Miscinski came charging over and asked Steve just what he thought he was doing. "You put me to sleep every day," Big Steve told him, "so I'm just making myself more comfortable."

Another time Miscinski really thought he had Steve in big trouble. He'd seen Steve in school earlier in the day and when history class began Steve was absent. Cutting a class meant automatic early morning penalty hours and Miscinski knew how much Steve hated getting up early, so he was grinning widely as he began calling the class roll. As Miscinski got to the B's—Big Steve's last name begins with an F—I saw the classroom door open and then close. Through the legs of the kids seated in the first row, I spied Steve crawling on his knees down the aisle toward the back of the room. Miscinski hadn't seen the door open and close. Those of us who had, however, and who watched as Steve stealthily made his way as silently and unobtrusively as possible toward his seat, did our best to stifle our laughter.

Just as Miscinski got to Steve's name on the roll and called it out, pen poised to mark him absent, Steve reached his seat, raised himself into it, and said in a loud voice, "Present, sir!" Miscinski slammed his attendance book down on his desk, his jaw dropped, his glasses fell off. "But you're not!" Miscinski yelled. "*You're* not here!" Big Steve just grinned at Miscinski while everyone in the room roared with laughter. Big Steve had done it again.

The ironic thing is that Steve really did like both Miscinski and the study of modern history. He just couldn't help clowning around. Now he's in the Big Time, and with all that advertising money at stake he can't afford to fool around quite as much. Big

Steve hasn't lost his sense of humor, however. The day before he was to leave New York for San Francisco we were talking on the telephone and I asked him, "What days do you want to go to the convention?" Steve just laughed and said, "None. We'll watch it on television."

Regarding politicians, Big Steve's point of view isn't too far removed from what King Levinsky, the former heavyweight fighter, remarked to my father in my presence in about 1954. "Dem guys," the King told my dad, "ain't none of 'em on da square. Dey can't be," said the King, "it's part of da job." King Levinsky, of course, was, like Big Steve, a Chicago boy. He gained a certain amount of notoriety by being knocked out on August 8, 1935, by Joe Louis. When I knew him I was a small boy and the King was selling hand-painted ties around the swimming pools of the luxury hotels on Miami Beach. According to the sports writer Ira Berkow—also a Chicago guy—the King claimed that Frank Sinatra once paid him a C-note for one of his ties; Al Capone, another of Levinsky's customers, donated fifty. The King was reputed to have made nearly a half-million dollars during his ring career, but he wound up punch-drunk and broke. What happened to the money? "Bad managers," said the King. "Dey're de only ones rottener den da pols."

As it turned out, Big Steve and I did attend the convention together. We went on Tuesday, the evening Jesse Jackson was scheduled to speak, figuring that it would be the most emotionally charged moment of a generally dull event. The overwhelming feeling of a political convention these days—for a so-called "objective" observer, that is—is staleness. Due to the proliferation of primaries, the most important issue—the choosing of a presidential candidate—is already decided, thereby relieving the affair of any genuine tension. Big Steve and I agreed that perhaps the last truly interesting political convention had been in 1960, when John F. Kennedy won the Democratic nomination.

While we waited through Speaker of the House Tip O'Neill's speech, and then the line-up of Rainbow Coalition members who introduced Jesse Jackson, Big Steve and I discussed what some previous presidents and presidential candidates might have done with their lives had it not been for several fortuitous twists of fate. Gerald Ford, for example, is easy to imagine as a tire-store owner in Kalamazoo, Michigan. "Friendly Gerry" would have been great doing ads on local TV, a guy you could depend on to suggest the right tires for your car, to guarantee the work. Friendly Gerry wouldn't have tackled anything too mentally strenuous; he would be conservative, but fair-minded, a responsible member of the community. Hubert Humphrey could have been the neighborhood druggist, taking over the pharmacy from his dad, a guy who wouldn't overcharge you for prescriptions. As vice-president, Humphrey had been obviously bent out of character when he backed LBJ all the way in the war in Vietnam. "And it came from the gut," Big Steve said to me. "He really believed in it."

Jackson's speech was a good one, he didn't hit a false note. He knew he had to be conciliatory and soft-pedal it or his career as a national politician would suffer. Jackson has modelled his machine after one of the best, Mayor Daley's, from the time of Martin Luther King's Operation Breadbasket, and he knows what it takes to survive. "Jesse looks like a stalking horse," Steve said. "He probably can't ever win, but he can clear the way for a more acceptable black candidate."

Watching Jackson gesticulate on the podium I remembered a night at a Golden State Warriors game in the Oakland Coliseum a couple of years before. The Warriors came running out and got a big hand—this is when they still had Bernard King and World

B. Free on the team—and then a few minutes later, while the Warriors were shooting around, warming up, Jesse Jackson and a companion entered the arena and walked to their seats in the front row. The applause he received was deafening, much larger than that accorded the Warriors, and Jackson stood and waved to the crowd. A guy sitting behind me turned to the man next to him and asked, "Who does *he* play for?"

NBC commentator Tom Brokaw reported that as Jackson came off the podium following his speech he asked one of his aides, "How did the Jewish thing go over?" (A reference to an attempt to reconcile his recently having called New York "Hymietown.") By that time Big Steve and I were on our way out of the Moscone Center. We'd sat through all but the final fifteen minutes or so of Jackson's speech in seats facing the podium, and then we went down to the NBC control booth to view the denouement. With forty pictures to choose from, the producers focused almost exclusively on people crying, holding children, those faces reflecting awe and rapture. These were, of course, genuine responses, but by no means did they represent the majority of the audience; they were, quite simply, the most sensational at the moment.

It felt good to get out into the cool night air of San Francisco. As Big Steve and I walked up Fourth Street toward Market, I recalled a definition of the word "democratic" I'd read earlier in the day in *Webster's New Collegiate Dictionary*: "Favoring social equality; not snobbish or socially exclusive." Earlier, before going to the control booth, Steve and I had attempted to enter a "hospitality" room in the NBC offices at the convention center to watch part of Jesse Jackson's speech on television, but we had been turned away. "Sorry," the guard at the door told us, "this isn't for NBC people—this is for government people." From the doorway I could see Jackson's sweaty face on TV and hear him speaking about breaking down the barriers between classes. Most of the "government people" had their backs turned to the television set and were nibbling on prawns or pieces of cake.

Once, sometime in the forties, King Levinsky was arrested for attempting to pick a guy's pocket at the bar of the Hotel Maryland in Chicago, a popular watering hole for visiting firemen just down the street from my dad's place. "You can't do this to me!" the King shouted at the cops as they took him away. "I'm a real American!" I've never been able to figure out exactly what he meant by that.

Death at the Ballpark

A fat guy fell out of the stands into the Kansas City Royals bullpen during the ninth inning of the seventh game of the American League Championship Playoffs at Exhibition Stadium in Toronto in 1985. I watched on TV as he lay there with his gut sticking out from under his shirt in a puddle of water while the Kansas City pitchers stood around looking at him and up into the seats and wondered how he got there. The guy looked dead. He wasn't moving and from 2,500 miles away through the miracle of electronic satellite transmission it looked to me like he wasn't breathing either. The Bluejays were behind in the game by four runs in the bottom of the ninth and it was obvious they'd blown their opportunity to meet the St. Louis Cardinals in the World Series when the fat guy landed on the field. It was several minutes before a medical crew reached the body but eventually four men managed to lift him onto a stretcher and carry him off through a door in the outfield fence.

The crowd was getting rowdy at this point because they knew the season was finished for their team. Not too many of them paid attention to the fat dead-looking guy. The TV cameras shifted suddenly from the bullpen to the Toronto Bluejays dugout. The players weren't paying much attention to the guy either; they sat staring at their shoes or their fingernails or just off into space, probably thinking about what they would say to their wives and kids and girlfriends when they got home. Undoubtedly some of them were wondering where they would be playing next year.

The incident reminded me of the time my dad and I were at a Chicago Bears football game at Wrigley Field on an ice-cold December day in 1956, when I was ten, and a fat guy carrying two large beers collapsed on the stairs in the aisle next to us. The beer splashed down the steps and froze, turning the snow green. The guy didn't even groan, he just lay on his back covering three steps like the man in the Kansas City bullpen did twenty-nine years later. My dad said to me that the guy must have had a heart attack or something and died on the spot because he wasn't moving.

Two Andy Frain ushers came running down the steps and looked at the guy. They tried to lift him up but he was too heavy; he kept slipping out of their hands but they kept trying to move him. He must have weighed close to three hundred pounds. Some fans seated behind us started shouting at the ushers to get out of the way, that they were blocking their view of the game. "Down in front!" the fans yelled. The ushers looked around helplessly. They were two tall skinny guys with bad complexions shivering in their short blue usher's jackets. Their ears were red from the cold, their noses ran. Nobody moved to help them. "Leave the guy!" someone shouted. "It's ten goddamn degrees below zero. He won't start stinking until June!"

Finally my dad and another guy got up and helped the ushers drag the dead man up the stairs to a landing where a third usher covered him with a blanket. This happened about midway through the third period. I kept looking back at the landing to see if they'd taken the body away but he was still there at the start of the fourth quarter. The game got exciting and I didn't check back again until just before the game ended and saw that the body was gone.

As we filed up the stairs on our way out of the stadium I looked over at the spot on the landing where they'd covered him up: there was nothing there but a patch of flat, dirty snow. The people around us were talking about the game, about the great catch Harlon Hill had made to put the Bears ahead, or the twisting, acrobatic forty-yard run the Detroit halfback Hopalong Cassady had made with a desperation screen pass. Most of the crowd didn't even know about the fat guy who had died on the steps by our seats. All they wanted to do was get into their cars and warm up.

The End of Racism

One of my favorite places to go when I was a kid in Chicago was Riverview, the giant amusement park on the North Side. Riverview, which during the fifties was nicknamed Polio Park, after the reigning communicable disease of the decade, had dozens of rides, including some of the fastest, most terrifying roller coasters ever designed. Among them were The Silver Streak, The Comet, The Wild Mouse, The Flying Turns, and The Bobs. Of these, The Flying Turns, a seatless ride that lasted all of thirty seconds or so and required the passengers in each car to recline consecutively on one another, was my favorite. The Turns did not operate on tracks but rather on a steeply banked, bobsledlike series of tortuous sliding curves that never failed to engender in me the sensation of being about to catapult out of the car over the stand of trees to the west of the parking lot. To a fairly manic kid, which I was, this was a big thrill, and I must have ridden The Flying Turns hundreds of times between the ages of seven and sixteen.

The Bobs, however, was the most frightening roller coaster in the park. Each year several people were injured or killed on that ride; usually when a kid attempted to prove his bravery by standing up in the car at the apex of the first long, slow climb, and was then flipped out of the car as it jerked suddenly downward at about a hundred miles per hour. The kids liked to speculate about how many lives The Bobs had taken over the years. I knew only one kid, Earl Weyerholz, who claimed to have stood up in his car at the top of the first hill more than once and lived to tell about it. I never doubted Earl Weyerholz because I once saw him put his arm up to the biceps into an aquarium containing two pirañhas just to recover a quarter Bobby DiMarco had thrown into it and dared Earl to go after. Earl was eleven then. He died in 1958, at the age of fourteen, from the more than two hundred bee stings he sustained that year at summer camp in Wisconsin. How or why he got stung so often was never explained to me. I just assumed somebody had dared him to stick his arms into a few hives for a dollar or something.

Shoot The Chutes was also a popular Riverview ride. Passengers rode in boats that slid at terrific speeds into a pool and everybody got soaking wet. The Chutes never really appealed very much to me, though; I never saw the point of getting wet for no good reason. The Parachute was another one that did not thrill me. Being dropped to the ground from a great height while seated on a thin wooden plank with only a narrow metal bar to hold onto was not my idea of a good time. In fact, just the thought of it scared the hell out of me; I didn't even like to watch people do it. I don't think my not wanting to go on The Parachute meant that I was acrophobic, however, because I was extremely adept at scaling garage roofs by the drainpipes in the alleys and jumping from one roof to the next. The Parachute just seemed like a crazy thing to submit oneself to as did The Rotor, a circular contraption that spun around so fast that when the floor was removed riders were plastered to the walls by centrifugal force. Both The Parachute and The Rotor always had long lines of people waiting to be exquisitely tortured.

What my friends and I were most fond of at Riverview was Dunk the Nigger. At least that's what we called the concession where by throwing a baseball at a target on a handle and hitting it square you could cause the seat lever in the attached cage to release and plunge the man sitting on the perch into a tank of about five feet of water. All of the guys who worked in the cages were black, and they hated to see us coming. Between the ages of thirteen and sixteen my friends and I terrorized these guys. They were supposed to taunt the thrower, make fun of him or her and try to keep them spending quarters for three balls. Most people who played this game were lucky to hit the target hard enough to dunk the clown once in every six tries; but my buddies and I became experts. We'd buy about ten dollars worth of baseballs and keep those guys going down, time after time.

Of course they hated us with a passion. "Don't you little motherfuckers have somewhere else to go?" they'd yell. "Goddamn motherfuckin' whiteboy, I'm gon' get yo' ass when I gets my break!" We'd just laugh and keep pegging hardballs at the trip-lever targets. My pal Big Steve was great at Dunk the Nigger; he was our true ace because he threw the hardest and his arm never got tired. "You fat ofay sumbitch!" one of the black guys would shout at Big Steve as he dunked him for the fifth pitch in a row. "Stop complaining," Steve would yell back at him. "You're getting a free bath, aren't ya?"

None of us thought too much about the fact that the job of taunt-and-dunk was about half a cut above being a carnival geek and a full cut below working at a car wash. It never occurred to us, more than a quarter of a century ago, why it was all of the guys on the perches were black, or that we were racists. Unwitting racists, perhaps; after all, we were kids, ignorant and foolish products of White Chicago during the 1950s.

One summer afternoon in 1963, the year I turned sixteen, my friends and I arrived at Riverview and headed straight for Dunk the Nigger. We were shocked to see a white guy sitting on a perch in one of the cages. Nobody said anything but we all stared at him.

Big Steve bought some balls and began hurling them at one of the black guys' targets. "What's the matter, grey?" the guy shouted at Steve. "Don't want to pick on one of your own?"

I don't remember whether or not I bought any balls that day, but I do know it was the last time I went to the concession. In fact, that was one of the last times I patronized Riverview, since I left Chicago early the following year and Riverview was torn down not long after. I don't know what Big Steve or any of my other old friends who played Dunk the Nigger with me think about it now, or even if they've ever thought about it at all. That's just the way things were.

A Place in the Sun

The final memory I have of my dad is the time we attended a Chicago Bears football game at Wrigley Field about a month before he died. It was in November of 1958, a cold day, cold even for November on the shore of Lake Michigan. I don't remember what team the Bears were playing that afternoon; mostly I recall the overcast sky, the freezing temperature and visible breath of the players curling out from beneath their helmets like smoke from dragons' nostrils.

My dad was in good spirits despite the fact that the colostomy he'd undergone that previous summer had measurably curtailed his physical activities. He ate heartily at the game, the way he always had: two or three hot dogs, coffee, beer, a few shots of Bushmill's from a flask he kept in an overcoat pocket. He shook hands with a number of men on our way to our seats and again on our way out of the stadium, talking briefly with each of them, laughing and patting them on the back or arm.

Later, however, on our way home, he had to stop the car and get out to vomit on the side of the road. After he'd finished it took him several minutes to compose himself, leaning back against the door until he felt well enough to climb back in behind the wheel. "Don't worry, son," he said to me. "Just a bad stomach, that's all."

During the summer, after my dad got out of the hospital, we'd

gone to Florida, where we stayed for a few weeks in a house on
Key Biscayne. I had a good time there, swimming in the pool in
the yard and watching the boats navigate the narrow canal that
ran behind the fence at the rear of the property. I liked waving to
and being waved at by the skippers as they guided their sleek white
power boats carefully through the inlet. One afternoon, though,
I went into my dad's bedroom to ask him something and I saw
him in the bathroom holding the rubber pouch by the hole in his
side through which he was forced to evacuate his bowels. He gri-
maced as he performed the necessary machinations and told me
to wait for him outside. He closed the bathroom door and I went
back to the pool.

I sat in a beach chair looking out across the inland waterway in
the direction of the Atlantic Ocean. I didn't like seeing my dad
look so uncomfortable, but I knew there was nothing I could do

for him. I tried to remember his stomach the way it was before, before there was a red hole in the side of it, but I couldn't. I could only picture him as he stood in the bathroom moments before with the pain showing in his face.

When he came out he was dressed and smiling. "What do you think, son?" he said. "Should I buy this house? Do you like it here?"

I wanted to ask him how he was feeling now, but I didn't. "Sure, Dad," I said. "It's a great place."

An Unsentimental Education

One typically blazing hot and muggy afternoon in the summer of 1959, when I was twelve and a half years old, my pal Vinnie and I wandered up to the A-rab's drugstore on 30th Street in Tampa, Florida, to get a Dr Pepper and browse through the skin magazines and cheap paperbacks that the A-rab stocked in rotating wire racks next to the soda fountain. I'd nicknamed the drugstore owner the A-rab because he had a scimitar-shaped proboscis and often wore a white towel over his head to absorb the sweat. At first I liked to imagine that the A-rab had fled Riyadh or Abu Dhabi in order to escape decapitation for having violated some powerful sheik's favorite daughter. He certainly looked the type; but after having gotten to know him as well as I did it seemed more likely for him to have violated the sheik's favorite camel. In reality the A-rab was a Jew from New Jersey who, like most snowbirds, couldn't take the bad weather anymore. He was a weird bird, though, with a really bizarre, sick sense of humor. I once named a pet alligator after him.

Vinnie and I often walked up to the A-rab's place to relieve the boredom of those long, unbearably humid days. We liked to sip our Dr Peppers and read passages to each other from such immortal sleazeball paperback classics as *Sin Doll* by Orrie Hitt, and *Four Boys, A Girl and A Gun* by Willard Weiner. On this particular afternoon, however, after first having been greeted by the A-rab in his usual genteel fashion ("Hey, kid, know why God in-

vented women?" "No, why?" "Sheep couldn't do the dishes."),
Vinnie or I plucked from the rack a faded-blue Gold Medal novel
by a man named Jim Thompson entitled *The Killer Inside Me*. "It
was too bad about Joyce Lakeland," began a quote from the first
inside page of the book. "If only she hadn't loved it when I beat
her, the whole trouble wouldn't have started." Obviously, Vinnie
and I agreed, we had stumbled onto something a little bit over the
border from *Sin Doll*. This Jim Thompson sounded like the
A-rab's kind of guy.

We killed the afternoon hanging out at the A-rab's reading the
Thompson novel. It turned out to be a strange, unforgettable
book about a small-town southern sheriff named Lou Ford who
specialized in *boring* people to death before actually murdering a
number of them. Ford's peculiar weapon was the platitude, clichés
repeated over and over ("every cloud has a silver lining") while his
victims, too frightened of Ford to run or rebuke, writhed in mute
agony.

Walking home Vinnie said something that startled me: "Your
dad was a killer, wasn't he?" "What do you mean?" I asked an-
grily. "Why would you think that?" "Oh, just something I over-
heard your uncle say to your mother one day." "What was it?"
"He was talking about Chicago," said Vinnie, "and why he left.
'You've got to be able to take care of somebody that needs taking
care of,' he said. 'Rudy knew how to handle that kind of stuff, not
me.' Something like that."

We walked the rest of the way without talking and after Vinnie
turned off to go to his house I cut through the old boat yard to the
river. I sat on the pier where earlier that summer my uncle had
skinned the hide off an alligator some cracker had shot for table
meat, and dangled my legs above the water. I thought about how
my dad was dead now, and I couldn't ask him if he'd killed
anybody. Nobody else could know for sure about something like
that, I figured. Nobody could ever know for sure.

Memoir of a Failed Cadet

My father never did any military service. I once asked him if he'd been in the war and he said no, that the Army hadn't wanted him. What he didn't tell me was that his arrest record disqualified him from the draft.

When I was in my third year of high school, bored as I was by school and suffering the usual adolescent blues, I briefly entertained the idea of enlisting in the U.S. Navy, going so far as to talk to a recruiter. Upon learning that the period of enlistment would be for a minimum of four years—then a full quarter of my life—I immediately dismissed the notion. I was not to escape entirely, however, the tentacles of the military establishment.

When I attended the University of Missouri at Columbia in the early sixties, before the anti-war, anti-military protests occasioned by mass student opposition to the Vietnam War brought to an end such requirements, male students were forced to enroll in one of the three branches of the Reserve Officer Training Corps (ROTC): Army, Air Force or Navy. Compulsory ROTC was an element of the basic agreement that established the University of Missouri as the first land grant college west of the Mississippi River.

I chose the Air Force for three reasons: 1. It was less populated than the Army and supposedly less rigorous than the Navy; 2. The uniforms were blue, my favorite color; and 3. My roommate,

Johnny Hugo of St. Genevieve, Missouri, was an Air Force ROTC Squadron Leader. This last reason was by far the most important of the three because as a Squadron Leader, Johnny—who was a junior, I was a freshman—was responsible for reporting attendance for his outfit, of which I made certain I was a member. I never attended ROTC, and since five absences from ROTC during a semester constituted automatic expulsion from the university, Johnny made sure that my name was never on the absent list.

Johnny did warn me that sooner or later I would have to show up. At the end of the year a parade of all ROTC forces was held by the columns of the university on a large grass field called The Quadrangle. This parade was attended by the governor of the state, several state senators and congressmen, and the president of the university. Johnny informed me that attendance was mandatory, that he would not be the one in charge of taking the roll. He advised me to go to marching drill at least a couple of times in order to learn the routines and formations so that I'd be able to acquit myself passably on parade day.

I, of course, blissfully ignored Johnny's advice, figuring that when the day came I'd have him give me a few pointers and I'd wing my way through the ordeal. I had no great enmity for the military; I chose not to attend ROTC drill simply because I felt I had better things with which to occupy my time: girls, books, sports, etc. I did not intend to become a soldier anyway.

Parade day, as Johnny had informed me, did eventually arrive, and I had at last to accouter myself in the military fashion. Johnny showed me how to properly tie my tie and affixed the silver eagles to the lapels of my coat. I cocked my flight cap at the regulation angle, spit-shined my shoes (I'd been wearing *them* regularly, anyway, because they were both durable and comfortable and I'd had to pay ten dollars for them—the rest of the outfit had to be returned at the end of the year), and prepared to confront the situation. Johnny cautioned me to make certain that I found a place in the middle of the group—that way, he explained, my missteps would not be so visible. He gave me a couple of quick lessons regarding flanking movements, which I just as quickly forgot, and then we drove together to the parade ground.

Once we'd arrived at The Quadrangle, Johnny wished me luck and went off to the officers' meeting place while I located "my" squadron. I carefully situated myself deep within the ranks and as the functions began I felt confident that I would be able to handle the maneuvers by faking my way along.

It was an extremely hot afternoon, better than 100 degrees on the bowl-like field. Almost as soon as all of the cadets were lined up preparatory to marching, several boys fainted and were carted off to the infirmary, there to be treated for heat prostration. The fellow next to me whispered out of the side of his mouth, "Happens every year. Some guys just can't take it. It's an easy way out but they keep you in the hospital for two days and give you a hard time." I briefly considered following suit but out of a kind of morbid curiosity about the affair decided to stick it out, despite the, by this time, horribly itchy woolen uniform and absurd conditions. I actually felt somewhat giddy about the whole thing. The thought of parading past the governor, the senators, congressmen and the president of Ol' Mizzou intrigued me.

I responded with a hearty "Here, sir!" like everyone else when my name was called by the Flight Leader, and waited at attention. The next thing I knew, the Leader had barked out a series of commands, resulting in the rearrangement of the squadron. Somehow, instead of my being buried back in the pack, in which position I had so skillfully placed myself, I was now first and foremost in the alignment, front left; the lead dog, as it turned out.

I was both horrified and amused, and I could not help but laugh. The Flight Leader, a diminutive student-colonel, strode over to me. The shiny black brim of his hat came up to my chin. "What's your trouble, Airman?" he yelled. His calling me "Airman" also struck me as being humorous and I fought to control my laughter.

"Are you laughing at me?" the Napoleonic colonel shrieked.

"No, sir," I said.

"At what, then?" he asked.

"Nothing, sir," I answered.

"It must be something," he insisted, sticking his skinny nose up into my chin.

I did not reply and looked straight out over his head.

"Did you shave today?" he asked.

I told him I had.

"You didn't do a very good job," he said. "There's a hair on your neck that must be an inch long! Look at that hair!" he ordered the boy to my right. "Wouldn't you say that hair is an inch long, Airman?"

"I couldn't say precisely, sir," said the boy.

"Good man," I said to myself.

"At *least* an inch long!" screeched the baby colonel. "Five demerits!"

I remembered something about this demerits business. If a cadet accumulated fifteen of them during the course of a semester he failed ROTC, and failure of ROTC constituted automatic expulsion from the university.

"Did you shine your shoes today?" he asked.

"Yes, sir."

"They're dusty!" he screamed. "Five demerits!"

"But we've been walking around the grounds, sir," I said. "They've just gotten dusty out here."

"Don't tell me what happened, mister!" he shouted. "That'll be four more demerits!"

I could hear several of my fellow cadets giggle.

"Quiet down!" the mad colonel squawked. "Or I'll hand everyone out here five demerits!" He returned his attention to me.

"And look at those eagles," he said. "They're crooked!"

I looked down at my lapels. The eagles looked all right to me.

"They're the way they're supposed to be, sir," I said. "Aren't they?"

I couldn't believe that Johnny Hugo had fastened them incorrectly.

"Are you telling me that I can't tell a crooked insignia when I see one, mister?"

"No sir, of course not, sir," I said. "It's just that they seem straight enough to me, sir."

"Not to me they don't!" he yelled. "Five demerits!"

I did a quick count in my head: five demerits for a bad shave, five for dusty shoes, four for insubordination and five more for the crooked eagles amounted to nineteen. I'd flunked out. I looked down at the heavily perspiring midget colonel and took off my hat.

"What are you doing?" he shouted. "Put your cap back on!"

"No," I said. "I'm through. There's no point in sticking around." I started walking away.

The little colonel hurried after me, yelling, ordering me to get back into line.

"I'm out," I said. "I'm gone. You can't tell me what to do anymore."

He didn't know what to do or say, so he trotted along beside me.

"But you *can't* leave!" he pleaded. "Not now, not in front of everyone on parade day!"

I laughed. "Watch me," I said, and kept walking.

Johnny Hugo ran over and asked me what the trouble was.

"The colonel here gave me nineteen demerits, so I'm out," I explained.

"He won't get back in line!" said the colonel. "He refused to march. Tell him to get back in place, Captain!"

Johnny knew better than to argue with me.

"Is it true that you gave this Airman nineteen demerits, Colonel?" Johnny asked.

"Well, yes," he said. "His eagles are on crooked!"

I should have said, "Like your head," but I didn't.

Johnny looked at my eagles and smiled.

"Then let's you and I get back to our troops, sir," Johnny said. "See you later," he said to me, and walked back to the parade line, followed reluctantly by the colonel. I went home.

Strangely enough, I did not fail ROTC. For some reason I received a passing grade. It wouldn't have mattered if I had failed, however, because I never went back to the university after that one year. Johnny Hugo became a flier and went to Thailand and Vietnam. He flew a number of combat missions but got out alive. The last I heard from Johnny, he was in the Foreign Service in Manila, where he'd learned to speak fluent Tagalog and had married a Filipino woman. I don't know what happened to the little colonel.

The military life, I decided, was not for me, so I managed to stay out of it, though I eventually worked a stretch in the Merchant Marine. I never did learn how to march.

The Brothers

I had always wanted a brother, and when my dad's second wife, Eva, had a boy, I was overjoyed. The problem was that we didn't live together and I didn't often get to see him.

Soon after my brother Willie was born, I wrote my first story. It was seven pages long, hand printed on yellow legal paper, and titled "All in Vain." It was about two brothers who don't know they're brothers. They fight on opposite sides in the Civil War and the Confederate brother kills the Yankee brother. After the war is over the Rebel brother discovers what he's done, gets drunk in a bar and dies in a gunfight.

Years later I was looking through my old desk at my mother's house for the story but I couldn't find it. I asked my mother what happened to it and she said she'd cleaned out the desk after I'd left home and thrown out everything that wasn't important.

Our dad died when Willie was six and I was twelve. After that I did not see my brother for ten years. When we finally did meet again we got along very well, and we continue to see each other regularly and to correspond. We don't, however, look at all alike. I'm medium tall and medium build with blue eyes and thick curly black hair, and my brother is very tall and thin with dark brown eyes and thin straight brown hair. Of the two, it's I who most closely resembles our father.

When we're together nobody ever guesses that we're brothers.

Whomever we tell invariably says how strange it is that we're so different looking. "We're half brothers," my brother or I say. "We had the same father."

I've always been sorry that Dad died without ever having been together with both Willie and me at the same time. As adults, I mean, or even as adolescents. It would have made us seem more like real brothers.

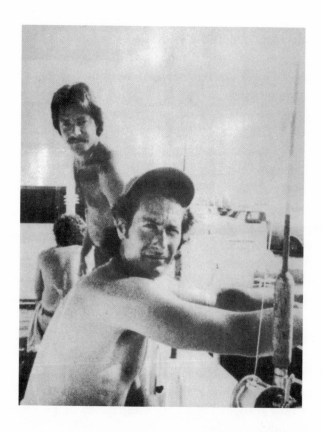

Listening to Willie

I went to see my dad's old friend, Willie "The Hero" Nero, who was now living in retirement in Las Vegas. A very old man, Willie nevertheless spoke with enthusiasm about the old days. I found that if I interrupted him, asked questions, it broke his train of thought and disturbed him. He knew why I was there and was willing to talk. All I had to do was listen.

"Your dad was a straight guy," Willie said. "I could always trust him to do whatever it was he said he'd do. No complaints on that score. Too bad he died so young, the future was his.

"Your dad never done nothin' really illegal that I know of, except maybe buying hot cases of booze now and again, or a ring maybe. The games never bothered nobody, the gambling, I mean. Look at all this, anyway, Vegas. A book is a book, you know? You got to pay off when you got to, otherwise it's yours. Everybody played back then. The cops knew it and let it be. Better than dope, you know? And the whores was somebody else's bailiwick.

"Rudy held onto things for people, he was good at keeping things in a safe place. People could trust him, plus he was a tough customer, he didn't take no shit never and he wouldn't rat. Two important points. Rare qualities for *any* business. *Any* business.

"I was always a soft guy myself. I wasn't much with a gun in my hand. I held one if I had to but what's the point? The real rough stuff was left to crazies, *meshuginas* such as Dago Mangano and

Dolf Valentino—'Kid Valentines' he called himself because he'd leave a valentine as a callin' card on the body. A psycho with a sense of humor.

"You know I was from the West Coast originally. Portland, where my old man ran a livery business. A taxi service with horses. I knew all about horses when I was a kid. Our name was Varshov, from Poland, Polish Jews. My parents couldn't wait to get out of there, the Polack anti-Semites. I was short—I still am—and pushy, so I got the name Nero, after the emperor, right? Even before I left Portland that was, before I went to LA. From LA I went to Chicago.

"Your dad was a kid when I met him. A bright kid, he went to college. You know that, I'm sure. That was rare, strange. He had an education but talked like he never been off Maxwell Street, Taylor Street. But you couldn't fool him, he was that way.

"One time we did something together. It was when your dad was startin' out. He came with me to Hollywood. I was sent because of my familiarity with the place. I'd lived there, as I told you, after Portland. We had some business with Zingermann, the old man, the father who produced all the big movies. He had a young wife who'd gotten in dutch and B. Z. Zingermann asked the boys in Chicago to help out. We did, then Rudy, your dad, and I, delivered her out to the old man. Look at me talkin' about an old man, now I'm older'n Zingermann was then.

"Anyway, we go out to LA and drop off the doll and B. Z. says stick around, learn the movie business. Have a holiday. So Rudy and I hang out for a few days, we gamble, at first it feels good in the sun with no overcoat, you know. One day we're on the lot and they're in the middle of makin' *Road to Fairyland*, with Little Ida MacFarland. She was a big child star who later killed herself as you probably heard. Cut her own throat one night, an unhappy kid. She was maybe nine years old when your dad and I were out there. So between scenes we go over to her trailer near the set there to see the old man. A flunky opens the door and there's B. Z. himself—'The Big Gun of Filmdom' they used to call him—stretched out on the couch with his pants down around his ankles while Little Ida performed as convincing an act of fellatio as you ever could hope to see.

"B. Z. never saw us, I don't think. He had his eyes closed and we backed off quick as we could. Ida saw us, though. She didn't miss a stroke, just raised one eyebrow the way she did all the time in the movies and stared straight at us for one solid moment before the flunky closed the door. B. Z. must have been in his seventies then.

"There never was anything nice about that Hollywood business. Your dad and I had a good laugh lots of times about that Ida MacFarland thing. I think after that we went down to San Diego on that trip, bought a warehouse to ship gum machines from or something. I don't remember.

"Just know your dad was no crook. If he cheated anybody they deserved it. This is a different world now and I don't mind knowing I ain't got a hell of a long time left in it."

Waking After Having Fallen Asleep
While Reading Rimbaud's
Les Deserts de L'Amour

I am puzzled but pleased by this dream. There was my father, dead
two dozen years, in a new flannel shirt and grey trousers, sitting
in the kitchen talking to me. There was activity in the kitchen but
I couldn't tell who else was there, they were blanketed in swirling
grey; women, perhaps, in maid's uniforms, rather old and bus-
tling about, as oblivious to us as my father seemed to them.

My father spoke softly to me, serenely, as if he had been away
and was soon to leave again, allowing us only this small conversation in an unrecognizable kitchen. He was much as I'd known
him the several years I had, and a child was what I appeared in
the dream, though I'd never remembered him so plainly dressed;
and his speech fell inaudible beneath the noise of the kitchen. I did
not mind the noise and stared straight at him, his body centered,
seated at the table, but spinning successively left to right, too, in
a semi-circle above me, drawing my attention away from the
words on his lips I was straining to hear. I did not, however, want
to push the moment; I felt satisfied with the time we had.

My father suddenly disappeared, leaving me alone at the table.
The kitchen was silent, black pans floating in frosty grey. My age

was now indeterminate. The dream turned over, revealing a prison visiting room, again grey and guarded by the others present, only more obviously so because of their badges and guns, guards of the prison.

Again I was seated, talking to my mother's fourth husband, through the mesh sheeting, though he could be plainly seen. He was happy, he told me, it was not that bad at all; he wasn't bothered by the need to please my mother, to make a living. The men inside were amiable enough, or did not talk; at least they left him alone. His cell was liveable, he said, and he did not mind the food. He had time to think and joke with the others. He was staying in, he said, until he understood why he was there.

The dream faded, and I was awakened by the crying of my baby daughter, as if her tears, elongated grey and silver, were rolling limp like mercury down the back of my neck.

The Favorite

It was my mother who introduced me to horse racing. She loved going to the track and often took me with her when I was a little boy. In Florida, at Hialeah, I loved to watch the pink flamingos pick their way among the fluttering green and yellow palms; and in Chicago, at Arlington Park or Sportsman's or Maywood, to listen to the heavyset, well-dressed men with diamond pinkie rings and ruler-length Havana cigars as they fussed over my mother, asking if she'd like something to eat or drink or if she wanted them to place a bet for her.

My father rarely, if ever, went to the racetrack. There may have been a bookmaking operation in the basement of his liquor store, but he told me that he didn't bet on anything with more than two legs that couldn't speak English. I doubt seriously if he'd ever heard of Xanthos, one of the two immortal horses of Achilles (the other being Balius) who had the power of speech and prophesied his master's death. If he had, I'm certain it would have served only to disaffect him further.

When I was in high school I became a real devotee of the so-called sport of kings. My friend Big Steve and I would often head for the track as soon as classes let out. Big Steve was a canny and gutsy bettor who won more often than he lost. Such was not the same in my case. I had as many off days as on and I always felt fortunate when I broke even. But there came a day I knew I couldn't lose. I was sixteen and Gun Bow, with Walter Blum up, was running in the feature race at A.P. I was certain there were no other horses in the eighth race that day that could beat Gun Bow, who was destined to be named Horse of the Year, beating out the great Kelso, a four-time winner of the award. The one problem for me was that I was broke at the time, so I had to borrow what I could in order to bet.

Big Steve was generous and loaned me twenty bucks. He was going through one of his periodic phases of gambling abstinence. Steve decided that he'd been gambling too much of late—horses, cards, craps—and he would test his willpower by refusing to bet on Gun Bow, even though he agreed with me that it was as close to a sure thing as there could possibly be. He even offered to drive me to the track and stand by me during the race.

Now, there are sure things and there are *sure* things. Gun Bow belonged in the former category. An example of the latter was the time my friend D.A. and I stopped before the first race to visit his uncle, Ralphie Love, who was working one of the ten-dollar combination windows in the clubhouse. Ralphie was a self-described "semi-retired businessman" who formerly had been in the vending machine business. He now worked part-time at the track and spent a lot of time attending sports events. I used to see him regularly at college basketball games in Chicago in the early sixties, especially before the game-fixing, point-shaving scandal hit. The day D.A. and I saw him at the track Ralphie told us he thought the five horse, Count Rose, would be a nice bet in the first race. The jockeys liked him, Ralphie Love said. D.A. and I bet the five to win, he went off at nine to two, and sure enough, just as the pack hit the top of the stretch they parted like the Red Sea and Count Rose came pounding down the middle to win by a comfortable margin. What I didn't know about Gun Bow was whether or not the jockeys liked him.

I borrowed a total of a hundred dollars and Big Steve and I headed out toward Arlington Heights. I intended to bet only the eighth, no other races, so we didn't have to be there until around three o'clock. Post time would be at approximately three-thirty. I'd place my bet, watch them run, cash in, go home. The sun was out, the road uncrowded. As Big Steve and I rolled along in his dusty red Olds a warm feeling of well-being engulfed me. I was so confident that Gun Bow would win in a breeze that I told Big Steve I was going to put the entire C-note on the nose, not across the board as I'd originally planned.

When we were about ten minutes from the track, the sky suddenly clouded over. Then a few drops of rain appeared on the windshield. Thunder rolled, lightning flashed. Seconds later we were inundated by a torrential downpour. Big Steve turned on the windshield wipers full speed but it didn't do much good. It was one of those sudden blinding midwestern summer rainstorms. "Oh no," I said, "I can't believe this." "Don't worry," said Big Steve, "we'll make it on time." "That's not what I'm worried about," I said, "it's Gun Bow. How does he run in the mud?"

I worried the rest of the way to the racetrack. By the time we pulled into the parking lot the rain had slowed to a steady drizzle but I knew the track surface would no longer be fast and I had no idea what effect sloppy footing would have on Gun Bow's performance. Due to the storm we arrived later than we'd figured to and I had to make a dash for the betting window.

I met Big Steve at the rail near the finish line. The rain had stopped entirely. "So," he said, "what did you do?" I showed him the two fifty-dollar win tickets. There were puddles on the track. The starter's bell rang and the horses were off. I recalled the time I'd picked a long shot named Miss Windway out of the paper one morning before Big Steve, his brother Big Lar and I went out to the track. I knew Miss Windway would win but by the time the

seventh race, the one in which she was entered, rolled around, I
was busted and had no more money to bet. I was disgusted with
myself for having lost everything so quickly that day and didn't
even bother to ask Steve or his brother for a loan. Big Steve, however, put six dollars across the board on Miss Windway, Big Lar
put two on the nose, and she went off at something like eighty-five
to one. Miss Windway won the race by five lengths.

Now, I figured, even though I had to bet more money to win
less, it was my turn. Gun Bow wouldn't let me down, he was too
good a horse to let a little mud bother him. Walter Blum was a top
jock, too; he wouldn't blow a big stakes race like this. As the
horses were moving into the far turn a guy behind us shouted,
"Do your job, Blum! I brought my gun with me today!" I turned
away and looked up at the sky. The sun came out. As the horses
reached the stretch an old guy next to me yelled, "Wa Wa Cy!
Come on, Wa Wa Cy!" The odds on Wa Wa Cy, I knew, were fifteen to one. I looked at the man. The top of his head was bald and
he was pulling hard with both hands at the small amount of hair
he had left above his ears. At the wire Gun Bow was in front by
three lengths.

On our way home Big Steve asked me what was the matter.
Why was I so quiet? I'd won, hadn't I? "Just thinking," I said. In
my mind I kept seeing that old guy tearing at his hair. "I don't
think I'll ever really be much of a gambler," I told Big Steve. "It's
foolish to bet long shots and no fun to bet the favorite." Steve
laughed. "You didn't see *me* betting," he said, "did you?" The sky
clouded over again and I closed my eyes. Wa Wa Cy, I thought,
how could that guy have bet on Wa Wa Cy?

The Fighters

Whenever I was sick at home in bed when I was a boy my dad would bring me comic books. Sometimes I was too sick to look at them but it made me feel better knowing that there were piles of comics next to me and on the floor by the side of the bed.

After the divorce my dad saw me only once or twice a week. We lived near each other, which made visiting easy, but he worked long hours and didn't really have very much time to spare away from his business. I understood this and since he and my mother were on friendly terms and spoke well of one another in the other's absence I had no difficulty in accepting the situation.

The time I was very sick with pneumonia Dad brought me a great many comic books—*Submariner, Superboy, Fantastic Four*—and sat by me on the bed and wiped my forehead with a cold washcloth. He kidded with me as he usually did, telling me I'd be up playing football in a couple of days, but he kept his voice down, that was different. He stood talking with my grandfather, my mother's father who lived with me and my mother, in the doorway of my room for what seemed like a long time.

Dad came over to me again before he left and picked up my hand. He looked at me until I opened my eyes. "Come on, boy," he said. "You remember Gumbo Roux, don't you? The welter from Morgan City?" I nodded yes. Dad had taken me to see him fight for the title at Graceland Arena when I was nine. "He had rickets when he was a kid," Dad said. "Pneumonia, too, every-thing. His family was so poor. And didn't he turn out okay! The way he snapped that hook on McKee."

I wanted to ask my dad what rickets were, but I was too weak to talk. He was grinning at me, remembering McKee coming up off his feet for a second, then flying left on his ear against the top rope before falling for good. "You'll be okay," Dad said. He squeezed my hand and my eyes closed again. I had an autographed picture of Gumbo Roux Dad had gotten for me—"To a Future Champ from The Champ" Gumbo Roux had written across his legs—but I couldn't remember where I'd put it.

I never saw my dad when he was sick, he wouldn't let me, and I didn't see him for several days before he died. My mother was going out one evening when she reminded me to call him in the hospital. She went out and I didn't call. The next afternoon, when I came home from school, my mother told me that my dad had died that morning. My grandfather, who had liked my dad very much, sat at the kitchen table, toast crumbs in his lap, staring into his teacup.

"You never called him last night like I told you to," said my mother. "Did you?"

I walked through the house into the living room and looked out the front window. Nothing was moving. I imagined my dad's big blue car coming down the street, Dad driving, a big cigar in his teeth, one hand on the wheel, the other right-angled out the open window, fingers gripping the roof. My mother came into the room and started talking. At that precise moment time began to pass more quickly.

Exile

We were led downstairs into a dimly lit room and invited to sit on fluffy, large pillows that were carefully arranged on the floor around a small, circular wooden table. Each of us was given a hookah and a bar of Lebanese tobacco, then instructed in the use of the hookahs and told that the smoking of hashish was not allowed.

The slab of tobacco was approximately the size of a bar of hotel soap. It glowed gold and red as I carefully inhaled and exhaled, establishing a comfortable rhythm with the water pipe. As my eyes grew accustomed to the dimness I saw that other people were distributed about the room on their own pillows, smoking and talking. The room was very large and glowed gold and red like the Lebanese tobacco.

The man who had led us in came back after a while and sat down next to me. He smiled and asked how we liked the tobacco and whether the pipes were drawing properly. He was very agreeable and told us how much he enjoyed living in London. He had been there twelve years now and he liked the people very much more than the weather. He entertained all sorts of people, he said, the most famous names in England. He started his own hookah and smoked with us for several minutes before excusing himself.

It had been raining hard when we'd come in and it was still raining when we walked out again into Fulham Road. The Duke hailed a taxi and once inside instructed the driver where to take us.

"Who is that man?" I asked.

"Don't you know?" said the Duke. "He's the chap that assassinated the King of Saudi Arabia in 1953."

The downpour increased in intensity and the cabbie began to swear. It occurred to me that in three weeks it would be Christmas. Today was the tenth anniversary of my father's death.

"Nice fellow, isn't he?"

"What?" I said.

"The chap there," said the Duke. "Nice fellow."

"Oh, yes," I agreed. He certainly had been very polite.

"Awfully damn nice," the Duke said, staring at the ribbons of water cascading down the window glass.

"Have you ever known anyone else who's committed a murder?" he asked.

"I'm not sure," I said.

"Well," said the Duke, "I daresay he must have had a handsome reason."

Riffraff

In the summer of 1984 I traveled to Chicago to see Louella Franklin. She was living in the White House, a well-to-do residence hotel on the Near North Side around the corner from the Seneca, the hotel I'd lived in with my mother and father until I was five years old.

Louella was a well-preserved seventy. She wore an auburn wig, her eyes were heavily made up, she wore red fingernail polish and plenty of jewelry. She smoked constantly—long, thin filter-tipped cigarettes—and sipped at a water glass filled with Johnny Walker Black Label. The voice was a surprise—rather than the throaty huskiness I expected, Louella spoke in a lilting, sing-song, exceedingly pleasant high register. When she smiled, which was often, she revealed even, sparkling white capped teeth.

"Riffraff," she said. "That's all any of them were. Oh, your dad was okay, he could be swell. Albert, too—he was a Good Joe. But Dago, a bum. Also that Strazza and Biaggi. Real scum. It was Willie Nero's boys knocked off Dago, you see. I'm certain of it. What he knew would have put any of them away, and times were changing, a new regime, you see.

"After I came to Chicago from New York, Dago and I went together for years, maybe ten. His wife knew about me, but she was smart, kept her mouth shut and took whatever she wanted. I never wanted to get married. What did I need that for? I was ahead of my time. Dago took care of me good most of the time, and when he was inside I had other friends. Dago didn't mind what he didn't know—what he didn't *want* to know, you see?

"Listen, all these guys were up to no good. That was their *business*! At least what the cops said was no good. It was no good only if they couldn't control it. You see? Dago was the one who took care of the problems, ever since Capone. He had the tavern—The Bomb Shelter—and they had food there, good food. That was his front, like Rudy had the liquor store. Some of them were in the trucking business, or warehouses, or had a couple stalls down on South Water Market. Everybody had a face to show.

"Rudy and Dago had a falling out, that's true. It wasn't too long after the Beau Jack–Jake LaMotta fight that Christmas. [Miss Franklin's memory is incorrect. Beau Jack, a lightweight, and Jake LaMotta, a middleweight, never fought on that or any other Christmas.] Between Christmas and New Year's it must have been. Dago and Rudy went to the fight together, at the Stadium, I think. The LaMotta fight must have been before Christmas, I forget the year. Forty years ago! I was still a kid then. The argument had to do with a bet on the fights. I know LaMotta won, by decision, so I guess it was supposed to have been a knockout. I don't remember who was supposed to knock out who, but because there wasn't a knockout there was something queer about the payoff.

"After that Christmas Rudy didn't come over to The Shelter and Dago didn't buy his liquor from Rudy anymore. It was too bad because I liked your dad. He was a generous guy, if he liked you. If he didn't, well—none of these characters really trusted anyone until after they'd done business with them. It was a tough world they made and you couldn't fake your way through it.

"I recall that Biaggi and Strazza and maybe Albert were involved in some kind of fencing operation. Maybe Dago, too. It was very clean except that Biaggi was always getting into too many things at once; that's what I heard, anyway. Spreading himself too thin. There probably was a case involving stolen bonds, I don't know. Nobody told me anything so specific, and I didn't want to know. What I didn't know couldn't hurt me, you see?

"They found Dago in the trunk of a car after he'd been missing for a couple of days. He'd been shot on Taylor Street and kidnapped. Nero had it in for him. Dago's wife and mother carried on something terrible. He had a mother like in a Jimmy Cagney movie, you know? 'He was a good boy, he always took care of me.' That kind of thing.

"Rudy ran around plenty in the old days, before your mother, during and after. For a long time it was with that blonde, Diane. She worked in the liquor store once in a while. Later I guess she took up with his pal, Albert. He was a sweet guy, actually, Albert. He had a thick accent; he was Cajun, a real one. His family, parents, brothers, sisters, still lived in shacks in the swamps down in Louisiana when I knew him. I don't know how he got into the rackets, but he handled a lot of business in New Orleans. He and Rudy were good pals. I think I heard Albert died about ten years ago.

"The one I admired most was Ginny Hill, Ben Siegel's girlfriend. When she told the government to go to hell. They never got a dime's worth of satisfaction out of her. She ended up in Switzerland, I guess it was, married to a ski instructor, before she died. She was a beauty, too, in her day, from Alabama. I always respected her attitude; what she knew was nobody's business but hers. That's the way I feel, too. I never said a good or a bad word I didn't want to."

Renoir's *Chemin Montant dans les Hautes Herbes*

The path on the hillside is a stripe of light, a three-dimensional effect. There is nothing theoretical about this: everything is where it is supposed to be. Not merely light and shadow and balance and color but the *unprepared for*, the element that informs as well as verifies the work. As the light in the Salle Caillebotte in the Jeu de Paume changes the painting changes, too—like the sun slowly emerging from behind a cloud, it opens and displays more of itself.

The people and the setting are from a previous century: women and children descending the path. There is absolutely nothing *savage* about the picture. Flowers, fruit trees, foot-worn path, wooden fence—nothing to disturb. The element of feeling is calm; difficulty disappears.

An early summer afternoon in the house in Chicago. I'm ten years old. The sky is very dark. A thunderstorm. I'm sitting on the floor in my room, the cool tiles. The rain comes, at first very hard, then soft. I'm playing a game by myself. Nobody else is around, except, perhaps, my mother, in another part of the house. There is and will be for a while nothing to disturb me. This is my most beloved childhood memory, an absolutely inviolable moment, totally devoid of difficulty. It's the same feeling I have when I look at Renoir's *Chemin Montant dans les Hautes Herbes*. I doubt very seriously if my father would have understood this feeling.

OBITUARIES

Obituary in *The Chicago Sun-Times*
December 5, 1958

WINSTON—Rudolph Aaron Winston of 6441 N. Ravenswood Avenue, dearly beloved husband of Eva; devoted father of James Barry and William Irwin; loving son of Ezra and the late Aura; dear brother of Bruno M. Winston and Irma Fox. Service Friday, 1 P.M., at chapel, 4300 W. Peterson Avenue. Interment Westlawn Cemetery. Member of Chicago Retail Liquor Association. Inf. Rogers Park 4-1150.

Obituary in *The Chicago Tribune*
December 5, 1958

Rudolph A. Winston, 47, of 6441 N. Ravenswood Avenue, owner since 1932 of the Lake Shore Liquor Store at 101 E. Chicago Avenue, died Thursday in Columbus Memorial Hospital. He was graduated from the University of Illinois in 1932 and was well known in Chicago for his participation in civic and charitable affairs. Survivors include his widow, Eva; two sons, James and William Winston; and his father, Ezra.

Item in *Chicago American*,
December 5, 1958

RUDY WINSTON, POPULAR RUSH STREET FIGURE, DIES

by Art Marx

Anybody who knows anything about what goes on in the city of Chicago knows that for the past twenty-five years much of that activity has taken place in and around the Lake Shore Liquor Store on the corner of Chicago and Rush streets. Now that Rudy Winston, the proprietor of Lake Shore Liquors, is dead, things are bound to be different. Rudy Winston's colorful circle of friends and acquaintances encompassed virtually every person of importance to live in or pass through Chicago during the past two and a half decades.

Politicians, movie stars, high rollers, low rollers, no rollers, thieves, murderers, show girls, junkies, bums, newspapermen and every cop in the city knew or knew of Rudy Winston. If you were out of pocket, and were an OK Joe, Rudy was good for a ten. If you needed a place to go for a while where nobody would find you, Rudy found you a place. Needed some publicity? Rudy made a call and the next day your name was in the gossips. He was on a first-name basis with the mayor, the governor, the Cardinal, the Capones.

Who was this guy, anyway, you ask? If you never got the chance to know Rudy Winston, all I can say is, I'm sorry. He was one of the guys who made this city go, and now he's gone too young. It's a shame, because Rudy Winston was a good man to know.

THE MORGUE

RACKET BOSS SLAIN

NEW YORK, Jan. 1, 1933— Johnny "Geronimo" Murphy, racketeer, ranking Public Enemy No. 3, was shot and killed tonight in his nightclub, Casa Blanca, on W. 65th St. He was slain by a doorman, Ted Mulrooney, whom Murphy had paid $100 a week, but recently had been forced to share his job—and pay— with another man.

Mulrooney called tonight to get his pay. Murphy met him in the soft-carpeted foyer hall. There was an argument. Three shots were fired. One bullet pierced the heart of the man who owned the bullet-proof car in which his girlfriend, Louella Franklin, was wont to do her shopping and make her calls. Mulrooney escaped and police have found no trace of him.

Murphy was 44 and had been arrested 44 times. He was convicted 37 times.

It was a Broadway legend that Ownie Madden, the city's leading racketeer, now in Sing Sing, got his start in the big profits that came in with prohibition when Murphy hired him, in 1923, to "protect" the Geronimo taxicab fleet.

Murphy was one of Broadway's smoothest celebrities. He had a weakness for indigo blue shirts and a high polish on the finger nails. Many of his intimates labeled him "racketeer," but he always said, "I'm a businessman."

* * *

MYSTERY MEN TAKE PASSENGER FROM TRAIN

CHICAGO, Feb. 20, 1940—Two men, one of whom represented himself as a detective from the Englewood Police Station, boarded an outbound Rock Island Train at the 63rd Street Station last night and compelled a passenger to get off the train and go with them.

The suspicion that the passenger might have been kidnapped was raised later when the Englewood police said that none of their men had been sent to meet the train.

The conductor said the supposed detective explained the passenger, whom the "detective" identified as

Anthony Strazza, was wanted for theft. The man did not protest much, the conductor added. One of the alleged kidnappers carried a pass issued to F. D. Foreman of Lebanon, Kansas.

* * *

BANDITS SLUG, ROB MAN ON NORTH SIDE

CHICAGO, July 3, 1943—Rudy Winston, cafe-society luminary, was robbed and assaulted yesterday by two strong-arm bandits, the police reported today.

Winston had just left the Rio Cabana, Near North Side night spot, when the bandits forced their way into Winston's Cadillac sedan as it stopped for a traffic light at Michigan Avenue and Delaware Place. Winston attempted to resist and was beaten around the head and face. Then the bandits ordered Winston to drive on. At 2640 Dayton St. Winston was relieved of $175. He was taken to Illinois Masonic Hospital where his injuries required four stitches.

Winston gained notoriety for a fracas earlier this year when he felled Milwaukee Ace brewery owner Edward Danillo with a right hook in the foyer of the Ambassador Hotel. Danillo refused to press charges and paid the hotel for damage caused to a plate-glass window.

* * *

MANGANO TROD ON TOO MANY TOES

CHICAGO, Aug. 5, 1945—The list of people upon whose toes Lawrence Mangano trod, at the cost of his life, was extended today to include gamblers in the 28th and adjoining wards.

Police were informed that Mangano sent out Johnny Bananas and Mouse Meehan to spread word he had the blessing of the political powers behind all Chicago gambling and that he was taking over West Side handbooks.

Some of the younger members of the Capone gang, who have postponed their debut as Public Enemies of 1945, had been collecting a 50% cut to provide "protection."

"Pops" Mangano sent sluggers to smash heads and handbooks, so the story goes, and aroused resentment.

The younger set sought to convince Mangano that the days of such methods were past, but he insisted upon setting up headquarters near Chicago Avenue and Pulaski Road. So they decided to reform him with bullets.

This was accomplished early Thursday, with Pop's bodyguard, "Big Mike" Pontillo, also being killed.

Pop's widow, Lila, a southern belle whom he married four years ago, added an angle to the case yesterday when she told police he was worried because FBI men were attempting to connect him with the high-jacking of cigarettes and a theft of $20,000 in bonds. Mangano had denied knowledge of either activity.

* * *

WIDOW BOLSTERS MANGANO CLUE

CHICAGO, Aug. 6, 1945— "Dago" Lawrence Mangano unwittingly kept his rendezvous with death at the hands of gangland assassins because he disregarded his wife's pleas to stay in hiding at their summer home.

Referring to him only as "Pops," the slain gambling-chief's widow, Lila, tearfully told Acting Capt. Louis Capparelli of the Maxwell St. station that, "Pops is dead today because he didn't take my advice."

Mrs. Mangano said she didn't know who killed her husband, "because I don't know of any enemy he might have had."

She said she and Mangano spent last Tuesday at their summer home at Lake Katherine in Lake County.

Tells of Hijacking

"He told me he knew he was in wrong with the government because of cigarette hijacking. He said he planned to come to Chicago the next morning.

"Tuesday night he got a call from a friend who told him he had better not show his face in Chicago because the FBI was looking for him.

"He said, 'The hell with them, they don't know who I am.' Much against my will I advanced him a large sum of money. I begged and pleaded with him not to leave me and our home for fear the 'G's' would get him."

Mrs. Mangano did not reveal the amount of money she gave her husband (according to police inventory, Mangano had only 92 cents on him when he died).

She said she last saw Mangano at 10:30 A.M. Wednesday, when he left for Chicago. She married him four years ago, she said. They lived at 57 E. Chicago, which is near The Bomb Shelter, a tavern reputedly owned in part by Mangano.

Mrs. Mangano, 35, a slender 5-foot, 2-inch redhead, was dressed in a black suit with a white blouse and a black velvet bow in her hair. She wore dark glasses during her questioning.

She was brought to the station by Ralph Cavaliera, 42, 2815 Dickens, in whose name Mangano's car was listed. Cavaliera was released from custody so he could contact Mrs. Mangano, whom police were unable to locate.

Suspect Victim "Squealed"

Mrs. Mangano's reference to cigarette hijacking served to bolster one of several theories being investigated by police in search of a motive for the slaying yesterday of Mangano and his man "Friday," Michael "Big Mike" Pontillo.

The hijacking theory had it that Mangano had "squealed" to the FBI in the theft and subsequent recovery of 126,000 packages of cigarettes consigned to overseas soldiers.

At the U.S. courthouse it was reported that the government was interested in this case as well as the theft of bond and liquor hijackings, but Mangano was only one of a score of suspects.

* * *

MANGANO DEATH TO GO UNSOLVED, DEMPSEY WARNS

CHICAGO, Aug. 6, 1945—Predicting that the Lawrence (Dago) Mangano murder will join the long list of unsolved Chicago gangland killings, John T. Dempsey, Republican nominee for state's attorney, vowed yesterday that as prosecutor he would drive protected crime out of Cook County.

"Hundreds of gangland slayings have given Chicago a bad reputation that is quite unnecessary," Dempsey said. He challenged the law enforcement authorities to clear up the fatal shooting of Mangano and a henchman but held out no hope they would, although they have an eyewitness.

Not a Conviction in Years

"There has not been a conviction obtained in a gang murder in years," Dempsey said. "Chicago has become known as the city where the underworld can kill and get away with it.

"Will the Mangano killing be solved? Will the murderers be tried? If so, will they be convicted? Certainly not, if the past is any indication of the future.

"Mangano is reputed to have been one of Chicago's gambling kings. He could not have conducted his extensive operations without the knowledge and protection of the law enforcement agencies of Chicago and Cook County.

"These agencies are all controlled by the Kelly Democratic machine. It will be interesting to see what motions these people go through now. If Mangano existed through their protection

and connivance, how far will they go in delving into the reason for his death?"

Gangsters Coddled, He Says

"How successful can they be, or do they want to be, in revealing all the circumstances surrounding his murder?

"The Kelly Democratic machine has been coddling gangsters for years because of their political value. Some of the real wheel horses of this machine are actually allied with the criminals.

"Crooked politicians supplying the protection are as bad as the gangsters themselves. During 365 days a year they are partners. They are partners, too, on the days when these murders occur.

End of Alliance Pledged

"When I take over the duties of the state's attorney's office, gangsters will be convicted. Investigation and prosecution will be vigorous, thorough and successful. The political-criminal alliance will be liquidated by honest, hard-hitting law enforcement. I will drive protected crime out of Cook County."

Dempsey and his campaign manager, Edward B. Casey, are vacationing in Wisconsin.

* * *

MANGANO'S ALGER-LIKE RISE

CHICAGO, Aug. 7, 1945—"Dago" Lawrence Mangano's "success story" goes back to 1911 when he went to jail as a panderer. From then on he rose swiftly from West Side brothel manager, police said, to West Side gambling boss, aide to Capone, and finally to his present state as sponsor of swank nightclubs and as a gambling king.

Through it all ran the theme of immunity, so much so that in 1931 Dago Lawrence boasted he had been arrested 600 times and never had been sentenced. He estimated that two years of his life had been spent in cells or courtrooms winning his release.

Starting well down on the list of 28 public enemies, Mangano climbed to No. 2 spot through his diligence in Capone's "syndicate" that boasted such characters as Frank Nitti and James (The Bomber) Belcastro on the general staff.

He was questioned in 1928 in the bombing of Police Capt. Luke Garrick's home; in the slaying of Rep. John M. Bolton in 1938; and the kidnapping of Sanitary Trustee John J. Touhy's son, John, Jr., in 1932.

When police sought a suspect in the murder of Estelle Carey, Colony Club dice girl found tortured and dead in her apartment where the slayer tried arson to cover the crime, they picked Dago Lawrence. Mangano was a silent partner in the Colony Club.

* * *

NAMES THREE IN MANGANO DEATH

CHICAGO, Aug. 8, 1945—An age-old gangland tradition was shattered last night when an underworld tipster gave police the names of three trigger men suspects in the assassination of Lawrence Mangano, ex-Capone mob biggie.

The names were whispered to Capt. Louis Capperelli of Maxwell Station by a veteran 42nd Ward hoodlum, who declared he was tired of paying tribute to, and being pushed around by, the racket syndicate.

He said the trio spent hours in Cicero late Wednesday and departed in a black sedan about the time Mangano left Ralph Capone's infamous Paddock Club in the suburb to keep his rendezvous with death.

Those sought are:

Dominic Nuccio, alias Libby, leather-skinned, pint-sized Near North Side gangster, reputed mob "enforcer" in the river wards, and his alleged torpedo men, Dominic Brancato and Dominic Bello.

Capt. Capperelli said the tip was a phenomenon in Chicago gang history. He declared it indicated clearly a brewing revolt by disgruntled factions against the Capone leadership.

He placed special credence in the information because, he asserted, Mangano had been muscling into gambling dives throughout the North Side and Nuccio believed a "finger" caused the raid on his place.

Mangano, who was in the wrong with the syndicate brain trust, and his bodyguard, "Big Mike" Pontillo, were fatally wounded by gunmen as they stepped from their car at Blue Island Avenue and Taylor Street. The gunmen then stuffed Mangano's body into their vehicle and drove off with it. Mangano was later found dead in the trunk of an abandoned car on South Prairie Avenue.

Police learned from Miss Consuelo Reyes, 24, who was riding with the victims, that the assassins had followed Mangano's auto from Cicero, but he thought they were policemen.

*   *   *

MANGANO RESTS IN A $10,000 PREWAR CASKET

CHICAGO, Aug. 9, 1945— "Dago" Lawrence Mangano lay in a $10,000 prewar silver casket yesterday as police sought the answer to his gangland murder, a secret which may be sealed with him in his grave.

Scores of mourners visited the Salerno Chapel at 813 Taylor Street, where funeral services for the slain former Capone chieftain are scheduled to be conducted at 9 A.M. tomorrow.

Only six floral pieces surrounded the casket. They included a heart of red roses from the widow and a broken wheel of assorted flowers. This traditional death offering to a gangster bore a card reading: "From the West Side Plant."

*   *   *

MANGANO SLAYING SUSPECT RELEASED

CHICAGO, Aug. 12, 1945— Dominic "Libby" Nuccio, 49, of 1003 Hudson Ave., Capone gangster and hoodlum, was discharged yesterday when he was arraigned before Judge William V. Daly in the South State St. Court. He was arrested Thursday for questioning in the Mangano murder and was charged with disorderly conduct when police found no evidence to connect him with the slaying. He denied being involved.

* * *

JURY REPORTS KILLERS OF MANGANO "UNKNOWN"

CHICAGO, Dec. 6, 1945— "Dago" Lawrence Mangano and Michael "Big Mike" Pontillo, gangland characters who were shot on Aug. 4 at Blue Island Avenue and Taylor Street, were killed "by unknown assailants," a coroner's jury, which recommended the inquest be closed, reported yesterday.

* * *

JOHN DILLINGER AIDE BEGINS 1 TO 10 YEARS IN PRISON

CHICAGO, Dec. 14, 1945—Samuel "Dummy" Fish, 42, said to have been a contact man for the gang headed by the late John Dillinger, was taken to Stateville prison yesterday to begin serving a 1 to 10 year term imposed in Criminal Court Nov. 26, 1942, upon his conviction on a charge of receiving stolen property. He was convicted of receiving $3,000 worth of stolen furs.

Rudolph A. Winston, of Chicago, arrested with Fish, was convicted as being an accessory to the crime and given a suspended sentence of 1 year.

* * *

WILLIE "THE HERO" WINS RELEASE AS SUSPECT IN VAULT ROBBERY

CHICAGO, April 17, 1946—Willie "The Hero" Nero, former Capone hoodlum, was plucked from Lake and LaSalle streets yesterday by a police squad and hustled to the Criminal Courts Building to be questioned about a $2,000,000 robbery, but he sauntered out a short time later, a free man because police admitted they had no evidence to warrant holding him.

Nero told Blair Varnes, assistant state's attorney, that he knew nothing about the Jan. 20 looting of the vault of the E. H. Rumboldt Real Estate Co., 624 W. 119th St. Before the grand jury he stood on his constitutional rights and refused to answer questions.

"I am a businessman," Nero told reporters after being released. "I own a bowling alley. I never robbed anybody."

* * *

FIND BODY IN CAR
ON WEST SIDE

CHICAGO, July 13, 1946—Gangland guns barked death here again today in what police called a burst of violence in the liquor black market.

The victim was Arnold "Suitcase Solly" Banks, 30, of 1300 Marine Drive, whiskey salesman and suspected operator in a liquor black market flourishing between Chicago and New York.

He was shot to death in an auto in front of 1622 Ontario Street during the night in a fashion reminiscent of Prohibition-day liquor wars. Banks' body, a bullet hole in his head, was found behind the wheel of his 1942 maroon Mercury sedan at 6:40 A.M. The motor was still running and the radiator was boiling.

Deputy Chief of Detectives Arthur Grant said: "There is a general belief that Banks was slain because others thought he had squealed, or was getting ready to squeal, about the black market."

Banks' pockets had been emptied of everything, and his wristwatch was missing. Three quarters lay on the seat, all that remained of the $1,000 he had collected earlier from Rudolph A. Winston, the proprietor of Lake Shore Liquor Store, Rush Street.

The victim's wife, Arlene, 26, former professional dancer at Colosimo's and other nightclubs, became hysterical when she learned of the killing. She refused to view the body.

"Suitcase Solly" went into the liquor business in 1941 as a salesman for the Blue Seal Liquor Co., a business, police said, owned and operated by Capone mob big shot Willie "The Hero" Nero. Nero is known to have been a beer boss during Prohibition days.

Banks is reputed to have gained his nickname of "Suitcase Solly" due to his having carried large amounts of cash from one location to another for the mob.

On Dec. 1, 1943, Banks was indicted with Maurice Goldberg, owner of the Spotless Distribution Co., 30 E. 88th St.; Pete Licavoli, a big figure in the Detroit rackets; George Prieto, another Detroit gangster; and Rudolph A. Winston, for distributing hijacked liquor. No convictions were obtained.

* * *

POET SUSPECT IN MURDER OF FORMER SHOWGIRL

CHICAGO, Dec. 16, 1955— Charles Wodarski, 27, of 32 S. Halsted St., a blond, blue-eyed poet, was seized by police yesterday for questioning in the investigation of the "lipstick murder" of Miss Diane Wood, 38, attractive former showgirl at the Club Alabam, Rush Street. Miss Wood was found shot and stabbed last Monday in her apartment in the Pine View Hotel.

The suspect was arrested at his home on an anonymous tip. Wodarski, who wears his hair unusually long, gave his occupation as a dishwasher. His pockets were filled with poetry, written on restaurant menu cards.

The poetry and other clues to Wodarski's handwriting were given to the police crime-detection laboratory for comparison with the writing which was found in lipstick on a wall in Miss Wood's room.

The suspect was asked by police to write the words on the wall: "For heaven's sake, stop me before I kill more."

As he complied, Wodarski said: "So that's what you want me for, to ask about the murder of the woman."

* * *

THE GULF COAST
BANK SNEAK

The Gulf Coast Bank Sneak

Since I was only twelve years old when my father, Rudy Winston, died, and he was in his late forties, I never really got to know him very well. The few facts I did have were related to me by friends and relatives, including my mother, in a vague, shadowy fashion. I was aware that he had been involved in various illegal activities, that many of his friends were gangsters and others whose businesses, according to my mother, were not strictly "on the up and up."

I wanted to discover more of the truth about his life, even if it was from an adversary source. I obtained the following material from the files of the Federal Bureau of Investigation in Washington, D.C., by request under provisions of the Freedom of Information–Privacy Acts. "The Gulf Coast Bank Sneak" case, as the FBI called it, originated at New Orleans, Louisiana, in 1945, and was registered as Chicago File no. 91–799. The reports were written and filed by federal agents investigating the case. The character of the case was Bank Robbery–Larceny–Conspiracy–Harboring, violations of the National Stolen Property Act, and involved a theft of $20,000 in bonds from a bank in New Orleans.

A note to the reader: This report contains raw F.B.I. data. No attempt at revision has been made.

* * *

At the time of Vincent Biaggi's arrest several persons who were in the Lake Shore Liquor Store at the time of the arrest were interviewed. Among the persons present was an individual who gave his name as Albert Thibodeaux. When questioned by Bureau agents Thibodeaux stated he did not know the person being arrested other than that he had seen him around the liquor store at one time or another. He stated he did not know Biaggi by name or his residence or business. Upon examination of Biaggi's Selective Service registration card it was ascertained he was registered from the Work House at St. Louis, Missouri, on June 3, 1942, and that he had given his home address as 3232 West Lafayette Avenue, Mobile, Alabama. He was 57 years of age. After it became apparent that this Biaggi was probably identical with the Biaggi mentioned in Bureau file #91–1244, efforts were made to locate him through the various hotels in the area near Lake Shore Liquor Store, with negative results. He was eventually located at the liquor store and apprehended there.

* * *

Rudolph A. Winston, the proprietor of the liquor store, and who was photographed and fingerprinted after Biaggi's apprehension, was interviewed on another occasion at which time he stated Biaggi had only been in the vicinity of the liquor store for possibly two days prior to his apprehension. Winston stated it was his impression that Biaggi was preparing to leave for Florida but was waiting for a friend to arrive. It is pointed out that Biaggi's automobile contained most of his luggage at the time, indicating his readiness for departure.

Special Agent Murphy ascertained there was no Star Liquor Company at the address given by Biaggi. The telephone number DELaware 2222 is assigned to the Lake Shore Liquor Store operated by Rudolph A. Winston, the scene of Biaggi's apprehension. Winston, who operates a retail liquor business, advised that Biaggi frequently purchased considerable quantities of liquor and then augmented those purchases by acquiring more liquor from other stores in the neighborhood and shipping it to Little Rock, Arkansas. Biaggi told Winston that he was a partner in operating a bowling alley at Little Rock. Winston stated further that he was certain that Biaggi was in Chicago on at least five occasions during 1944 and visited his liquor store in company with a female companion. This is contradictory to the statement made by Louella Franklin that she was not in Chicago during 1944. Little Rock was advised of the above by teletype dated January 13, 1945.

Following the apprehension of Biaggi, Special Agent Murphy interviewed Rudolph A. Winston who advised that he had operated a liquor store for the past 17 years. He stated he knew Biaggi under the name of Robert Towns for about the past year. He said Biaggi/Towns hung around the liquor store so frequently that he began helping wait on customers during busy hours. He said Biaggi/Towns always carried a big roll of money with him but never had any associates other than a female companion whose name Winston could not recall. He said Biaggi/Towns frequently received long distance telephone calls from Mobile, Savannah, Atlanta, Little Rock and New York over the private phone in the liquor store, DELaware 2222. He never received any mail at the liquor store, however.

* * *

Other persons in the liquor store at the time of the apprehension were Dwayne Black, a clerk, who knew nothing, and Arthur Stolowitz, a delivery boy for the liquor store, who stated he knew nothing. On a subsequent interview by Special Agent Murphy, Arthur Stolowitz admitted that he had given Biaggi a ration check drawn on the Halsted Bank in Chicago for the amount of 4,000 red points. [Red points were ration coupons distributed during World War II by OPA, the Office of Price Administration.] This check was later found in the possession of Biaggi when he was apprehended. It was dated January 4, 1945. Arthur Stolowitz stated that he had on previous occasions given 200 or 300 red points to Biaggi, for all of which he received no remuneration, and that he did it in order to ingratiate himself with Biaggi. According to Stolowitz, Winston had informed him that Biaggi was a "big shot" and could be used or useful to him on subsequent occasions. The incident concerning the red points was brought to the attention of the OPA in Chicago by Special Agent Murphy.

* * *

No indication Rudolph Winston or Lake Shore Liquor Store, Chicago, engaged in narcotic traffic or that Winston engaged in criminal activities with Biaggi. A check of the records of the Chicago Police Department failed to reveal any criminal record for Dr. Michael Leary. Leary advised that he resided at the Knickerbocker Hotel in Chicago and that he was not acquainted with anyone by the name of Biaggi and that a check of his records failed to reveal that he had ever had a patient by that name. He also said that he knew nothing about Rudolph Winston, and that he had never done any business at the Lake Shore Liquor Store, 101 East Chicago Avenue. He was unable to explain how Biaggi might have obtained his phone number, and stated that it might have been through some other patient of his. He stated that it was possible that some of his patients might have done business at the Lake Shore Liquor Store.

Louella Franklin stated that no one by the name of Al Star had ever contacted her regarding narcotics or liquor sales. She further advised that she knew nothing about Rudy Winston or the Lake Shore Liquor Store.

Donald R. Worthy, Narcotics Bureau, Treasury Department, Post Office Building, Chicago, Illinois, advised that a check of his records failed to reveal that he had ever received any complaints indicating that Rudy Winston or the Lake Shore Liquor Store had been engaged in narcotic traffic. He further stated there was no indication that Dr. Michael Leary might be involved in any narcotic violation. He stated that a check of the American Medical Journal revealed that Leary was a specialist in internal medicine and was an associate professor of medicine at the University of Chicago. Worthy also checked his records against the names of Vincent Biaggi, Albert Thibodeaux and Al Star, with negative results.

He stated that he knew of Albert Strazza as a big narcotics operator in the New York area, but that he did not know of any connection Strazza had in Chicago. He said that his files do not contain any information on Strazza.

* * *

Albert Thibodeaux advised that he knew Rudolph "Rudy" Winston as the owner of the Lake Shore Liquor Store. He said that at the present time he is in the restaurant business in New Orleans, Louisiana, and in Chicago, Illinois. He said that he bought liquor from Rudy Winston at the Lake Shore Liquor Store and he became rather well acquainted with Rudy Winston and his business activities. He stated that he knew Vincent

Biaggi by the name of Towns. He said that Anthony Strazza, who used to be the cigar clerk and the cashier at the liquor store, was a friend of Biaggi's and that Biaggi used to drop around to see him at the store. He said that it was through Anthony Strazza that Biaggi met Rudy Winston. Thibodeaux advised that Anthony Strazza was a nice fellow, but that he had become involved with "Dago" Lawrence Mangano in a shooting on the North Side of Chicago at one time. He advised that Anthony Strazza was no longer at the Lake Shore Liquor Company. Thibodeaux denied knowing that Anthony Strazza was the brother of Albert Strazza, a reputed organized crime figure in New York City.

Thibodeaux said that after Biaggi had been around the store for a while he got to using Winston's private phone in the store, and finally got to helping out in the store behind the counter and that Winston was apparently glad to have him because help was very hard to get at that time. He said that Winston and Biaggi were friendly and went out to dinner together a few times, but that he had never seen anything indicating that they had ever engaged in any business transactions of any kind. He said that Biaggi told him that he had an interest in a bowling alley in Little Rock, Arkansas, that Biaggi used to buy liquor and send it back to Arkansas, and that Winston had on a few occasions sold Biaggi some liquor.

He advised that he had never heard of the Star Liquor Company, 97 East Chicago Avenue, and that 97 East Chicago Avenue was a fictitious address. He advised that Winston had a liquor license, but that he had never seen any activities indicating Winston used the Star Liquor Company as a front of any kind. He said that it was his opinion that Biaggi had used this name to ship liquor to Arkansas in order that his presence in Chicago could not be traced.

Anthony Strazza said that during the time Vincent Biaggi would come to the liquor store a man whom he knew only as "Al" would often come in and visit for an hour or so with Rudy Winston. On viewing the photos of Alonzo Stella, Strazza positively identified him as the party he knew as "Al." "Al" was usually accompanied by another individual whose name he could not recall. He described this third party as from fifty to sixty years of age, five-feet, five-inches, 125 pounds, slight build and gray hair. He said that this party was usually drunk. He said it had been his impression that "Al" and this third party were close friends.

He said also that it was his impression that "Al" usually stayed either at the Palmer House or the Bismarck Hotel when he was in Chicago. He advised that the last time "Al" came to Chicago, Biaggi and this third party were also in Chicago. He stated that as he remembered Biaggi was supposedly living somewhere on the South Side of Chicago. He stated that at this time Rudy Winston was living at the Knickerbocker Hotel. He said that Rudy Winston had apparently made arrangements at the Knickerbocker to get "Al" a room there. He advised that he did not know if "Al" stayed at the Knickerbocker or not, and suggested that perhaps "Al" stayed at Biaggi's place on the South Side. He said that he did see this third party on one occasion in the lobby of the Knickerbocker Hotel. He said that as far as he knew Winston was never too friendly or too well acquainted with "Al" and that he was not as close to him as he was to Biaggi. He said that from what he knew of Winston's activities he did not think that Winston was involved in any criminal activities with Biaggi.

Strazza said that he thought Winston was all right, but that he was inclined to cut corners rather close at times. He said that he knew for a fact that Winston had been offered hijack liquor from time to time, but that he had refused to touch it. He said that as far as he knew Winston's operations had always been okay, but that Winston had recently purchased a fur coat which had turned out be hot. He said that during the time he worked at the Lake Shore Liquor Store there never were any indications that Winston was involved in narcotics violations.

Strazza said that Winston had resided at the Knickerbocker Hotel until three weeks ago when Winston married the daughter of the McCloud Railroad Company family, and that they were at the present time residing at the Seneca Hotel on Chestnut Street.

Strazza said that he had never seen "Al" at the liquor store or elsewhere since the time Biaggi had been apprehended. He further advised that he had never seen anyone similar to the photo of Louella Franklin in the company of Vincent Biaggi. He said that the photograph of Louella Franklin in no way resembled Diane Wood, who is presently employed at the liquor store. He advised that Wood hasn't enough brains to operate with Biaggi, was dumb, and has loose morals. He stated that he never heard Winston speak of Louella Franklin and he had never heard or seen anything indicating that Winston had any questionable connections in New York.

* * *

Diane Wood said Alonzo Stella used to come to the liquor store quite often, and Stella is inclined to do a lot of talking, likes to bet on horses, but she had never seen anything indicating he had any criminal connections in Chicago. She said that Stella met Biaggi at the liquor store, and that she did not think he had any other contacts with him except at the store.

A check of the records of the Chicago Police Department failed to reveal any criminal record for Diane Wood.

Wood stated that Winston and Stella appeared rather friendly, but that she knew of no transactions that they had ever handled together. She advised that "Dago" Lawrence Mangano operated The Bomb Shelter Tavern directly across the street from the Lake Shore Liquor Store, and that she had heard that Mangano and Rudy Winston had been friendly at one time, but that they had had an argument over something or other and that "Dago" never came to the store as he formerly did. She advised that she knew nothing concerning the connection between Mangano and Anthony Strazza. She advised that she did not know where Alonzo Stella lived during the time that he was in Chicago, and stated she could not recall a short, elderly man who was usually drunk as having been in the store during the times that Stella was there. She said that she could not recall Winston ever having spoken of Albert Strazza of New York and knew of no contacts, business or otherwise, that Winston might have in New York.

* * *

It is to be noted that the Lawrence J. Mangano, alias "Dago" Lawrence Mangano, FBI No. 732125, referred to above, was a prominent racketeer in Chicago, having been arrested over 200 times on charges of pandering, mayhem, kidnapping, alcohol running, bombing, murder, etc. Mangano was slain in a gang killing on August 3, 1945.

Albert Thibodeaux advised that he goes to the Lake Shore Liquor Store at least once a day when he is in town, and he knew Biaggi apparently was friendly with Winston but was not officially employed by him. He stated he had no idea why Biaggi

used the address of Anthony Strazza, which was a building operated at one time by "Dago" Lawrence Mangano. He said to the
best of his knowledge he had never been in the building. Thibodeaux does not recall ever having any business dealings at
any time with "Dago" Mangano.

* * *

Anthony Strazza advised that he knew "Dago" Mangano operated the building at 41 LaSalle Street. He stated that he knew
Albert Thibodeaux at the Lake Shore Liquor Store, but that he
could not make an identification from the picture of Hyman
Slivka as anyone whom he had ever seen in the store. He said
that Vincent Biaggi had used the LaSalle Street address without his permission in order to obtain some ration books. He
said that Biaggi later told him that he had done so, and asked
him if the ration books had come. He stated that some other ten-
ant of the building had gotten the books and that they were
turned over to Biaggi. He stated that neither Biaggi nor Alonzo
Stella had ever been in or lived in his rooming house.

* * *

Arthur Stolowitz stated that he had been employed as a delivery
boy at the Lake Shore Liquor Store for a year and a half. He
stated that "Robert," whose last name he did not know, was a
customer at the liquor store. He said that Robert occasionally
helped Rudy Winston in the store putting stock on the shelves,
helping at the cigar counter, etc., but that he did not think that
Robert was paid by Winston. He further advised that he did not
think Robert and Winston were particularly close friends. He
stated that Robert always came to and left the store alone, ex-

cept for one occasion in January of 1945 just a few days before
the arrest. He said Robert was arrested when returning to the
store after a vacation, and was accompanied by a man who was
slightly taller than he was and about five or ten years older. Stolowitz was unable to recognize pictures of Louella Franklin
and Alonzo Stella as ever having been in the liquor store. He advised that he did not know where Robert resided, but was certain that he had never lived at 41 LaSalle Street, the residence
of Anthony Strazza. He advised that a man who resembled the
picture of Hyman Slivka, taken November 29, 1941, generally
hangs around the gas station on the southwest corner of Chicago and Franklin between 12 and 1 P.M. He described this man
as follows:

Age	45 to 50
Height	6 feet
Weight	160 to 170 pounds
Dress	Dressed in work clothes
Peculiarities	Might have a slight limp

He described this man as often accompanied by a man whom he
described as follows:

Age	In his fifties
Weight	160 to 170
Height	5 feet, 4 inches
Build	Heavy
Hair	Brown
Glasses	None

Stolowitz advised that he had never seen either of these men in
the liquor store nor in the company of Robert. He stated that he

did not recall anyone named Star or Stella, and that he was not acquainted with Louella Franklin.

Spot surveillance was conducted at the corner of Chicago and Franklin with negative results as to anyone who resembled Slivka. Stolowitz advised that a man who somewhat resembled Alonzo Stella except that he was shorter used to come by the station and catch a streetcar at the corner. He advised that he was under the impression that this man was a salesman and was employed somewhere in the neighborhood. He stated that he had never seen him accompanied by any other individual.

* * *

Diane Wood, a part-time clerk at the Lake Shore Liquor Company, 101 East Chicago Avenue, advised that she knew Alonzo Stella only as a frequenter of the liquor store, and that she knew nothing about him or his associates. She was unable to identify the picture of Hyman Slivka as anyone that she had ever seen in the store. It is to be noted that she is not identical with the picture of Louella Franklin.

* * *

Lake Shore Liquor Company, Inc., was chartered in February, 1932, with a paid in capital stock of $20,000 and a moderate surplus. The store is the outgrowth of the individual enterprise of Rudolph A. Winston at the location. The store has had moderate success and has met its obligations promptly.

A check of the records of the Chicago Police Department Revealed negative results as to criminal records for Diane Wood, Arthur Stolowitz and Dwayne Block.

The following is the criminal record of Rudolph A. Winston, FBI #322954:

Contributor of Fingerprints	Name & No.	Arrested or Charge Rcvd.	Disposition
Prob. Unit, Chicago, Ill.	Rudolph Aaron Winston, #——	8-10-32	Violation of N.P.A.
U.S. Marshal Chicago, Ill.	Rudolph Aaron Winston, #——	8-11-32	N.P.A.
PD, Chicago, Ill., Prob.	Rudolph Winston #D-22959	3-17-42	R.S.P. 1 Yr.
BFD, Chicago, Ill.	Rudolph Aaron Winston, #99–799	Inquiry 1-16-45	

* * *

Rudolph A. Winston, 101 East Chicago Avenue, advised that approximately two years ago Vincent Biaggi first came to the store to visit with Anthony Strazza, who at that time was employed by him as cashier and cigar-counter clerk. He stated that it was through Strazza that he met Biaggi, whom he knew as Robert Towns. He said that Biaggi used to hang around the store quite a good deal, used the phone and received phone calls, and finally helped out behind the counter, but was never employed by him. He said that Biaggi spoke of owning bowling alleys in Arkansas and Alabama, and said that he intended to build one in Chicago. He said that Biaggi claimed to have an income of $100,000 a year and always carried a large amount of money on him, sometimes as much as $20,000. Winston estimated this from the fact that Biaggi would have enough $1,000 bills to riffle them. He stated that he never knew where Biaggi lived until he made arrangements for him to get a room at the Knickerbocker Hotel at Biaggi's request. He said he was under the impression, however, that Biaggi always stayed at the better hotels in Chicago.

He stated that one of Biaggi's friends, Alonzo Stella, known to him only as "Al," usually called at the store to see Biaggi when he came to Chicago. He advised that this might have been anywhere from a few days to a month after Biaggi first came to Chicago, and "Al" began to regularly show up at the store to see Biaggi a few days after his returning to town. Winston advised upon viewing the photograph of Hyman Slivka that he was the man known to him as "Slick." He denied that he knew Slivka before being introduced to him by Alonzo Stella and said he was never very well acquainted with him. He said that Al and Slivka were very friendly and he was under the impression that they would live at the same place because on occasions Biaggi would relate that he had to get a room for Al and Slick.

Winston said that when Biaggi first began coming to the store a man known to him only as the "Old Man" used to come to see Biaggi. He described this person as always drunk, slovenly in appearance, about sixty-five years old, five-feet, four-inches tall, and partly bald. He said that he had not seen this party for some time, and that he did not think he was in Chicago at the time Biaggi was apprehended. He advised that he did not think Biaggi was particularly friendly with "Dago" Lawrence Mangano, who operated The Bomb Shelter across the street from the liquor store, although he and Biaggi had dinner there on a couple of occasions.

He said that at one time Anthony Strazza had been employed by "Dago" Mangano, but that they had had a falling out, and that at that time Strazza began work for him. Winston said he fired Strazza in about August of 1944 because he was not doing his work and spent too much of his time playing the horses. He said that during the time Strazza was employed in the store he and Biaggi used to go out together quite often. He advised that after Strazza left he did not know whether Strazza saw Biaggi and that Strazza never came to the store. Winston stated that he knew "Dago" Mangano had been murdered at about the time he fired Strazza but he did not recall whether or not Biaggi was in Chicago at that time. For the record, "Dago" Lawrence Mangano's body was found in the trunk of an automobile on South Prairie Avenue on August 3, 1945. It is believed by the Chicago Police Department that his death was the result of a gang dispute, and no suspects were taken into custody in connection with that killing.

Winston advised that Albert Thibodeaux had been an old customer of his for many years and that he comes into the store quite often. He stated that Thibodeaux used to go out with Diane Wood and he was under the impression that Thibodeaux and Wood had taken some trips together inasmuch as Wood would relate that she was going to see Albert Thibodeaux and then would be gone for a week or so. He recalled that on the night that Biaggi was apprehended, Thibodeaux and Wood came to the store together. He recalled Biaggi having previously said that he was arranging to get a room at the Knickerbocker for Al and Slick and that he had asked Thibodeaux about getting a room in that or another hotel. Winston advised that he had never seen Alonzo Stella and Hyman Slivka together at the Knickerbocker, that he had never been in Stella's room there, and he knew nothing about Stella's activities. It is to be noted in reference to the report of Special Agent Murphy dated January 30, 1945, that inquiry made by Special Agent Murphy revealed that Vincent Biaggi, using the name Robert Towns, had made arrangements to obtain a room at the Knickerbocker Hotel for "Mr. Straight" of New York City, who was to come to the hotel on January 9, 1945, but he never appeared.

Winston stated that he had never seen anyone resembling the picture of Albert Strazza in the store with Vincent Biaggi or Alonzo Stella. He stated that Biaggi spoke of knowing people in New York, but that he had never mentioned any names and that he could not recall his having spoken of an Albert Strazza or a Mr. Straight. He further stated that he had never heard of the Star Liquor Company. He stated that Biaggi had received quite a few phone calls from New York, some from a man named "Al," but advised that he did not know the nature of this association and that Biaggi made no remarks to him in this regard. He stated that Alonzo Stella received no phone calls or mail at the Lake Shore Liquor Store.

* * *

Thomas P. Quinn, manager of the Knickerbocker Hotel, 163 East Walton, stated that Rudy Winston had stayed at the hotel from July 19, 1944 to January 23, 1945. He stated that he was unable to find Winston's bill for the entire period, but he had been able to ascertain that from July 19, 1944 to September 18, 1944 Winston had made no long distance telephone calls.

* * *

Arthur Stolowitz stated that he regularly reported to Rudy Winston on Tuesday and Friday nights to get his orders. He stated that he was present the night Vincent Biaggi, whom he knew only as "Robert," was apprehended by the FBI. He stated that he had become casually acquainted with Robert, who used to hang around the liquor store, and from whom he got tips on the horses. He stated that Robert told him he had a bowling alley in Little Rock, Arkansas, and that he spoke of opening a big alley in Chicago. He said that Robert asked him for some red points for himself and his wife and also for some for the bowling alleys, and that inasmuch as he thought Robert was a big shot and that he might benefit in some way if Robert opened a bowling alley in Chicago, he gave them to him.

* * *

Albert Thibodeaux, in a third interview conducted by Special Agent Murphy, confirmed that he was talking with Vincent Biaggi at the time Biaggi was apprehended. He stated that there was a tall, well-dressed man also present at that time whom he thought someone had referred to as "Cy" or "Sid," but that he could not make an identification of this party as the same man as Alonzo Stella's picture. He stated that he had never seen this man before the night Biaggi was taken into custody. He emphatically denied that he had ever known Alonzo Stella or anyone resembling the photo of Alonzo Stella.

He stated that he was acquainted with Vincent Biaggi, had seen him in the liquor store on different occasions, and had gotten tips from him on the horses, but that he did not know of any business dealings Biaggi might have had outside of a bowling alley and his liquor purchases. He further advised that he did not know of any business deals conducted by Rudy Winston and Vincent Biaggi and Winston at The Bomb Shelter of "Dago" Lawrence Mangano.

It is to be noted that Special Agent Murphy can testify that Albert Thibodeaux was in the Lake Shore Liquor Store, 101 East Chicago Avenue, when Vincent Biaggi was apprehended there on January 8, 1945. The records of the Illinois Liquor Control Commission, 160 North LaSalle Street, failed to reveal any sort of liquor license ever having been issued to the Star Liquor Company, 97 East Chicago Avenue.

Albert Thibodeaux, of 601 Napoleon Avenue, New Orleans, Louisiana, and presently of the Ambassador Hotel, Chicago, Illinois, denies that he knew anything of Biaggi's activities in Chicago, but that he knew Biaggi must have had a racket of some kind, just as he knew Anthony Strazza had a racket because he was receiving only $20 a week for working for Rudy Winston. He advised that all three of them used to play the horses, but that he never questioned Biaggi as to his source of income. Thibodeaux denied that he and Biaggi had ever made any trips together, and stated that Biaggi never mentioned any of his contacts in or outside of Chicago and he never heard him mention any names. He further advised that he had never heard Biaggi speak of Alonzo Stella and stated that he had never heard of anyone by that name. When questioned as to how he knew that Anthony Strazza received only $20 a week from Rudy Winston as a salary in the Lake Shore Liquor Store, Thibodeaux responded that Winston told him that if he paid him more Strazza would just throw it away on the horses.

*　*　*

Diane Wood stated that she would see Albert Thibodeaux off and on when Thibodeaux was in Chicago. She denied knowing of any business dealings he may have had with Rudy Winston or "Dago" Lawrence Mangano. She stated that about a year ago "Dago" Mangano had a fight with Rudy Winston at the Lake Shore Liquor Store, and that he had not been in the store since. She advised that she had heard "Dago" Mangano had been knocked off and found in the trunk of a car, and that she probably had learned this information from the newspapers.

She said she could not identify the picture of Albert Strazza as anyone she had ever known or seen in the store. She denied knowing where Vincent Biaggi lived in Chicago or who his associates in Chicago might be. She said that she had been informed that Rudy Winston had put the finger on Biaggi, causing his apprehension. She said it was through Winston that Thibodeaux had met Biaggi, and that Winston was the only person knowing his address. She said that she had been told that the charges against Biaggi had been dismissed at New Orleans, and she said that if Biaggi were taken back to Little Rock on a murder charge she felt that he would beat the rap inasmuch as it was apparently an old charge and she understood that Biaggi had good connections in Little Rock. When asked how she had formed this opinion she stated that she only knew what she had heard around Winston and Thibodeaux. She advised that she had not seen Anthony Strazza since he was fired from his job at the Lake Shore Liquor Store.

Confidential informant D—— stated that he would attempt to ascertain if Rudolph Winston had made any contacts in New York since March 2, 1944, at which time he was observed in the company of Samuel "Dummy" Fish, a suspected associate of various New York City organized crime figures. It is also interesting to note that in the report of Special Agent Murphy in the instant case, it is reflected that Rudolph A. Winston was very close to Alonzo Stella, both of whom are in the liquor business. Stella has associated with persons who are in the liquor business and also known bond fences in New York, some of whom are also narcotics dealers, such as Albert Strazza. It appears possible that the Lake Shore Liquor Store in Chicago is also engaged in narcotics traffic. It appears that there is a possible connection between Rudolph Winston and Albert Strazza, who was involved in extortion and contract murder with Willie "The Hero" Nero, a well-known Chicago gang figure, and with "Dago" Lawrence Mangano. It is believed that Willie Nero and Rudolph Winston shared a proprietary interest in a bookmaking operation conducted from the Lake Shore Liquor Store in January and February of 1944, and that Strazza acted in concert with them in unidentified business deals.

A further interview will be conducted with Winston in connection with the Gulf Coast Bank Sneak. Above information should be borne in mind and information should be sought from Winston bearing on that case. Will likewise make an appropriate investigation at the Knickerbocker Hotel to determine whether or not Biaggi was registered there since a review of the reports from the Chicago Division in the Gulf Coast Bank Sneak reflects that Winston was to make a reservation for Biaggi under the name of Robert Towns at the Knickerbocker. An attempt will be made to set a definite period of time as to when Biaggi and Alonzo Stella were seen together at the Lake Shore Liquor Store since such is important for the purpose of establishing both Biaggi and Stella's movements.

All offices conducting investigations in the instant case should keep the New York Field Division advised of developments and should furnish them with copies of reports.

Louella Franklin refuses to have anything to do with any law enforcement officers and further efforts to make an appointment with her were futile. She requested that any interview be conducted by telephone and stated she would terminate any conversation if she felt the questions were inappropriate.

She was questioned by telephone concerning her knowledge of the activities of Vincent Biaggi, Alonzo Stella and Albert Strazza, but declared that she had never heard of any of these three persons. She did admit that she was acquainted with "Dago" Lawrence Mangano, and at one time regularly associated with Willie "The Hero" Nero, who she claims to have met through Mangano. She said that at no time was she privy to any conversation between Nero and Mangano regarding business activities.

She advised that she knew nothing of the Lake Shore Liquor Store other than that it was across the street from "Dago" Mangano's Bomb Shelter and that if she had met Rudy Winston she could not now recall having ever done so. She stated that she had only a passing acquaintance with employees and patrons of The Bomb Shelter Tavern and knew none of "Dago" Mangano's friends outside of Willie Nero, nor was she familiar with any of Mangano's business dealings.

Since it was obvious that Franklin was uncooperative and did not choose to admit any acquaintances with the pertinent subjects in this case, the interview was terminated.

Dwayne Black stated that "Dago" Lawrence Mangano had had a fight with Rudy Winston in the Lake Shore Liquor Store and that he had not been in the liquor store since. He was unable to identify the picture of Alonzo Stella as anyone he had ever known or seen in the store during the time he had been employed as a clerk. He denied knowing where Vincent Biaggi lived in Chicago or knowing who his other associates in Chicago might be. He identified Albert Thibodeaux as a friend of Rudy Winston's and said that he knew only that Thibodeaux was in the restaurant business. He stated that he had heard of Willie Nero, had seen his picture in the newspapers, but had never met him or seen him in the liquor store.

On October 3, 1945, Rudolph A. Winston was interviewed by the writer at his place of business, the Lake Shore Liquor Store, Chicago Avenue and Rush Street. Winston stated at this time he had been thoroughly interviewed previously by Agent Murphy and other agents of the Chicago office and that he had given them all the information about this case that he had in his possession. Winston stated that altogether he had probably seen Vincent Biaggi and Alonzo Stella together in the Lake Shore Liquor Store four or five times. The last time was on the night of Biaggi's arrest. The last time before that, he stated, was five or six months prior to Biaggi's arrest. Before that he stated it had been a year since he had seen Biaggi. He stated that he had seen Stella several times before that but did not know he was in any way connected with Biaggi. Winston advised he knew nothing specific of Biaggi's business dealings.

Winston denied that he knew anything of Willie "The Hero" Nero other than what he read in the newspapers. He stated that he had not seen "Dago" Lawrence Mangano since they had a falling-out regarding the sale of liquor by the Lake Shore Liquor Store to Mangano's Bomb Shelter Tavern. Winston said he knew nothing of the circumstances of Mangano's death other than what information had been made available through the newspapers. He stated he did not think that Albert Thibodeaux had been acquainted with "Dago" Mangano or that Thibodeaux had been acquainted with Willie "The Hero" Nero.

At this point Winston stated that he had no further information to offer on any subject and thereupon declared the interview over.

LIST OF ILLUSTRATIONS

Barry Gifford was born on October 18, 1946, in Chicago,
Illinois, and raised there and in Key West and Tampa, Florida.
He has received awards from PEN, the National Endowment for
the Arts, the Art Directors Club of New York and the
American Library Association. His writing has appeared in
*Punch, Esquire, Cosmopolitan, Rolling Stone, Sport, The New
York Times, The New York Times Book Review,* and other
publications. Mr. Gifford's books have been translated into
fifteen languages, and his novel *Wild at Heart* was made into
an award-winning film by David Lynch. He lives in the San
Francisco Bay Area.

Cover design by Russell Chatham.
Book design by Stacy Feldmann and Jamie Potenberg.
Composed in Sabon, Times Roman and Clarendon
by Wilsted & Taylor, Oakland.
Printed and bound by Arcata Graphics, Fairfield.

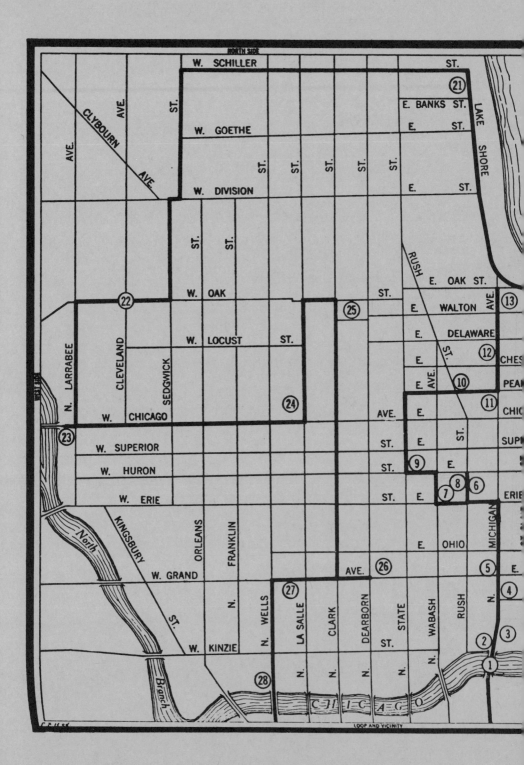